A REQUIEM OF SHARKS

Also by Patrick Buchanan

A PARLIAMENT OF OWLS
A MURDER OF CROWS

A REQUIEM OF SHARKS

Patrick Buchanan

A Novel of Suspense

DODD, MEAD & COMPANY
New York

ISBN: 0-396-06841-3
Library of Congress Catalog Card Number: 73-7488
Printed in the United States of America
by The Haddon Craftsmen, Inc., Scranton, Penna.

For Margaret and Ken Millar,
two lovely people by the sea

A REQUIEM OF SHARKS

1

WHEN I saw a shark's dorsal fin cut the smooth surface of the pool, it sent a shiver up my back. Despite what they print in the publicity designed to convince you how wonderful beaches are and how meek and docile is your average shark, I reached the conclusion early in my skin-diving training that I would gladly let sharks have as much of the ocean as they want.

But finding a shark in a swimming pool? *That* was surprising.

What was more surprising was the red-haired girl who dashed from the house and jumped right into the pool along with the shark. I got my mouth open to yell a warning, but it came out as a senseless croak.

Miss Redhead was stark naked.

When she first ran out of the big house, she didn't see me. Her eyes had a vague look to them. The rest of her was worth looking at twice. But she didn't give me that much time. That was when she turned and leaped into the pool.

Charity Tucker, who had seen the shark too, screamed "Look out!"

"Get my gun," I yelled and, as I heard her start for my car, I ran to the edge of the pool and looked for something to throw.

It was unlike any swimming pool I'd ever seen before. It was sunk deep in the ground and, at one end, there was a large pipe leading out toward the beach. The shape was circular, with no corners. A ladder leaned on the curve nearest the house, and the naked girl seemed to be trying to make her way to it. But the shark was in the way.

"Don't splash around!" I called. "Tread water."

The shark made a swift circle around the girl. I threw a lawn chair toward him, hoping to attract his attention. He ignored it and moved closer to the girl. I couldn't be sure if she had heard me, or even if she was aware of her danger.

Then, for the first time, she saw the shark. She clawed at the water and screamed.

"Don't splash!" I yelled again. She didn't hear. She frothed the water in her panic. I threw another chair. The shark wasn't stupid. He knew aluminum isn't good to eat, and naked redheads are.

I grabbed a long-handled skimmer, the kind they use for raking leaves out of the water, and took a mighty swing at the shark. He was faster than me, and got out of the way. The momentum stumbled me to the pool's edge where I completed my stupidity by skidding on a wet spot and falling in myself.

2

Now there were two of us in the water, plus one large and apparently hungry shark.

I tried to remember my shark survival training. Come to think of it, I hadn't had any such training. My survival technique up to now had been to stay away from them.

I vaguely remembered that the experts warned against splashing around. Such gestures remind Mr. Shark of frightened schools of fish, and tend to provoke him to attack. What else? Don't panic. The experts said that, too. I wished I had an expert with me right now. Then I could flail the water with *him,* while. . . .

Well, one thing the experts recommended stuck with me.

Get the hell out of the water.

Good idea. I swam backwards toward where I thought the naked redhead might be, not daring to look away from the shark. Over my shoulder, I said, trying to keep my voice steady, "Swim toward the ladder. Slowly."

Then something went BLAM! and a geyser of water shot up just in front of my nose.

My lovely partner, Charity Tucker, had nearly plugged me with my illegal .38 Police Special.

"Don't shoot!" I shouted. Charity is a wonderful girl, but she cannot hit the inside of a barn with a pistol. She scared me almost as much as the shark.

She also scared the redhead, who suddenly grabbed me from behind and started trying to climb up my back. That pushed my head under water and I didn't expect it, so I inhaled a couple of gallons of water and started thrashing

3

around and making noise and doing all the things the experts recommend against.

The shark came over to see if I had been transformed into a nice school of mullet. When he got close enough, I kicked him in the snout and almost broke my ankle.

Two things happened after that. The redhead let go of my neck and started swimming for the ladder. And Charity tossed the pistol to me. Naturally, it fell short and sank. I made a dive for it, but it was just out of reach.

I broke the surface for air and dove down again. This time I got the pistol and as I swam topside, I saw the shark moving toward me. I didn't dare fire the gun under water —it would have exploded like a hand grenade. And before I was in a position to use it, the shark made his move. He came in at me fast, starting to roll to one side. I kicked furiously and tried to go the other way. He hit me a glancing blow with the middle of his body and it was like being run over by a tank covered with sandpaper. I got the gun up against him and fired one shot that threw water all over and bruised my hand with the recoil, and then I saw his tail whipping toward me and it was at that moment that the sky fell.

2

SINGING RIVER, MISSISSIPPI, is on the Gulf Coast halfway between Mobile, Alabama, and New Orleans. On the map, they give it one of those little "0" markings, the one they use for towns with a population of less than 1,000. When we drove over the causeway, Pascagoula was ten minutes behind us, and Gulfport was somewhere up ahead, in case you ever want to find the place.

I have already mentioned Charity Tucker. She is very beautiful and very blonde and very stubborn. She is also a very bad shot with a pistol. But she has a mind that absorbs and stores information like a computer.

Charity is the Tucker of "Shock and Tucker—Investigations." I am the Shock half—Benjamin Lincoln Shock. Until a few weeks back I was a New York City cop with the unpopular notion that lawbreakers shouldn't be ignored or pampered just to keep down the noise. But that is another story. And a sad one, as anyone who has been to a big city recently can tell you.

Anyway, without really intending it, I found myself in

partnership with Charity Tucker. Despite the exploits of Mike Shayne and Shell Scott, there's no such beast as a tough, gun-packing, crime-solving private eye. Not any more, and I doubt there ever was. Local cops are very itchy about their territory, and not too friendly toward outsiders who come in trying to make them look bad. How would you like it if some guy followed you around on the job, second-guessing you and getting in the way?

Also, there is the little problem of licenses. A private detective licensed in, say, New York, can't legally work in New Jersey, just across the river. And let us not forget all the agitation about weapons these days. In New York, you need a license just to buy a handgun, and getting permission to pack it is like asking the governor to lend you his wife. As a result, very few private individuals carry pistols in the Empire State, except for the criminals, of course, who, being criminals, have a notorious disrespect for picky little laws. Which is a long-winded way to explain that the .38 Police Special I carry is illegal as hell, and that "Shock and Tucker—Investigations" is equally so.

But sometimes people find themselves in a situation where official law enforcers can't or won't help. That is when the telephone rings in Charity's tiny Madison Avenue apartment. Once a day, wherever we happen to be, she calls her own number and when it rings, Charity puts a little electronic beeper up against the mouthpiece. Whereupon a mysterious recording machine hooked up to her New York City phone plays back all the messages she's gotten in the past twenty-four hours. I don't pretend to

6

understand how it works, but Charity is loaded with such electronic gadgets, and they intimidate me.

Two days ago, we had been in Gethsemane, Kentucky, trying to help a college friend of Charity's. Maybe we were unlucky, maybe we were inept, but the friend died and it didn't ease any of the discouragement for us when we caught the killer. You do what you can, and sometimes it isn't enough.

I didn't want to be in this line of work anyway. But Charity called her automatic phone and the next thing I knew, I was driving my big old Cadillac Fleetwood south toward the Gulf of Mexico and Singing River, Mississippi.

We had left Pascagoula behind, driving west on Route 90. A tiny crescent moon with a peculiar corona halo around it swam through the darkness of the sky.

"I don't like that," I told Charity. "The last time I saw the moon look like that was one night on a Marine amphib operation off Vietnam. A sudden storm came up and we lost three of our LSTs."

I switched on the radio and, after sweeping the dial through a barrage of Hank Williams records, found a news broadcast.

I'd been right. The announcer was reporting the weather.

"Tropical Storm Hilda has not yet been classified as a hurricane," he said, "but already winds up to sixty miles an hour have been recorded in Montego Bay." He assured us that the weather service was keeping a careful watch on Hilda, and would let us know exactly what to expect if we would only stay tuned to WPMP in Pascagoula. I told him I would, if he'd give us a little Peggy Lee along with the Hank Williams, but he must have misunderstood, because he immediately put on "Jambalaya."

"This Christmas," promised Charity, "I'm going to give you one of those cassette decks so you can stop complaining about the radio."

"I don't think you'll be able to find one that would work in this heap," I told her. "This car's so ancient it has a six-volt electrical system."

"So we'll hook up a transformer," she said smoothly. I couldn't tell if she meant it or not. You can never be sure with Charity. What she doesn't know about electronics could be stashed safely in a gnat's eye.

We passed a green and white sign that said, "Welcome to Singing River, Miss. Pop. 502."

"This must be the place," I said. We were on a long causeway. It was a narrow two-lane bridge, built low and near the water. On one side, a wooden platform extended along the railing to keep bridge fishermen out of reach of the speeding traffic.

I was not in the best of moods. My head ached where a Kentucky herb doctor named Uncle Uglybird had put a row of stitches in to counteract a slight case of dangling scalp I'd gotten from a car wreck on our last case. I am fond of my Fleetwood with a bond that goes further than that which usually exists between man and machine. But my behind ached, too, from almost five hundred miles of driving since dawn.

8

"I don't see why we couldn't have pulled in at that nice-looking Holiday Inn back in Pascagoula and looked up our client in the morning," I grumbled.

"Our client said she'd put us up at The Old Place," Charity told me.

"That's what worries me. The Old Place sounds like one of those shacks where Jefferson Davis slept on his march to the sea. Or was that Stonewall Jackson?"

"It was Sherman," Charity said. "Cheer up, Ben. We're almost there."

"Says who?" I said, staring ahead into the darkness. "Are you sure we didn't make the wrong turn and this isn't the overseas highway to Key West?"

"There's a light up ahead," she said.

I saw it—a cold white glare on the edge of the bridge. I slowed.

"Watch out for headlights behind," I said. "I don't want us to get clobbered by some sleepy truck driver."

I stopped at the light. It was a double-mantled Coleman gas lantern, hissing and throwing out the equivalent of a two-hundred-watt bulb. A burly man leaned over the edge of the catwalk with a cane pole. I got out of the car and he turned around. His black face glistened in the harsh glare of the lantern.

"Something wrong, mister?"

"No, just information."

Suspiciously, he asked, "What kind of information? Are you one of those Yankee newspapermen?"

"Not a chance. We're just passing through. And we

9

wanted to look up a friend. She's staying at a house called The Old Place. Can you point us toward it?"

He hesitated, considering. "Won't do no harm," he said finally. "You're pointed right. Stay on Ninety until you pass the yellow blinker light. Then make your first left turn and drive down to the beach. You can't miss it. It's a big old house with white pillars. And if that ain't enough, it's right beside a lighthouse."

"You said *light*house?"

He nodded. "Big white one. Don't no light burn in it any more, though. Not since the war."

I got back in the car. "Thanks."

He kept staring at me. He started to say something, then stopped.

"What is it?" asked Charity.

"Well, ma'am," he said slowly, "if I was you folks, I'd be mighty careful about driving up to The Old Place unannounced. They don't like strangers around there."

"Thank you very much," she said, turning on her considerable charm. The fisherman didn't have a chance. His knees melted the way any normal man's would, and he turned back to his cane pole mumbling to himself.

I slowed down when we came to the end of the bridge. We were passing through the outskirts of Singing River.

It was like most of the small Mississippi coastal towns we'd seen. Low, flat buildings set back well off the highway, under scraggly pine trees. Small shopping centers with neon Piggly-Wiggly signs and 6-hour Martinizing dry-cleaning shops. A couple of taverns with Jax Beer signs lighting the windows.

"I wonder what Jax Beer tastes like," I said. "We ought to check it out."

"Later," Charity said firmly.

We came to the yellow blinker and I slowed to a crawl. I'd noticed that the side roads weren't marked very well along route 90.

"Just ahead," said Charity. "Past that church."

I put on the turn signal and turned left. The Fleetwood slid noislessly past the old Baptist church and its graveyard filled with tilted headstones and statues of holy angels.

The road led to a gate flanked by two brick columns. It was open. But a few yards inside, a roadside sign read NO TRESPASSING.

"Maybe our friend the fisherman was right," I said.

"We're expected," said Charity. "The message was for us to go straight to the house and ask for Miss Lisa Dantzler. The message came through her lawyer, and he was explicit in his instructions. We were not to stop in Singing River, or to make any more of our presence than we could avoid."

"In other words," I said, "Miss Dantzler doesn't want anyone to know she's brought in the pinch hitters."

Calmly, Charity said, "That's the name of our game, Shock."

"I see the lighthouse up ahead," I said. "Who the hell

11

would build a house right under a lighthouse?"

"According to my Welcome to Mississippi brochure," Charity said, "it was the other way around. The house was owned by a New Orleans shipping baron. The Old Place was his summer house. One night, back in the 1880's, one of his ships went aground on Ship Island. When the town of Singing River wouldn't spring for a lighthouse, the good baron built his own."

"A *private* lighthouse? Well, why not? It makes as much sense as owning your own private jet plane."

"There's the house," said Charity.

It would have been hard to miss it. Mansion is the closest word I could think of, and I wasn't sure even that was grand enough. Remember Tara in *Gone with the Wind*? White pillars in front, and enough windows to give the handyman a double hernia just washing them all. A circular drive covered with white seashells swept gracefully past the front door.

"Are you sure this place isn't some kind of museum?" I asked. "Who the hell could afford to heat it?"

"You're not in New York now," Charity said. "This is the deep south, remember? It's warm down here."

"Well, it looks like somebody's at home. The lights are on and I wouldn't want Miss Dantzler's electric bill, either."

We pulled up in front of the pillars and got out. It was a little like strolling up onto the front porch of the White House. I pressed the doorbell and heard chimes inside. We waited.

12

No one came.

"Try again," said Charity.

I did, and the chimes tinkled. But that was all we heard. No closing of doors, no sounds of footsteps.

"I thought we were expected," I said.

"Let's go around back," Charity suggested. "Maybe they're having a barbecue or something."

"In a place like this?" I grumbled, leading the way. "If you'd said banquet I might have bought it. Besides, I don't smell charcoal."

The back yard, if you could call it that, was well-lighted, too. There were comfortable chairs and tables and sun umbrellas arranged around a circular swimming pool. Beyond it, the beach was a white ribbon in the moonlight and the surf made phosphorescent splashes in the Gulf.

An odor of magnolia hung heavy in the air. The breeze off the Gulf cooled the sweat on my forehead.

Looking around at the flood-lit pool area, I said, "Nice way to live. If you can afford it."

"You lived too long in Manhattan," Charity told me. "Anybody who has a back yard looks rich to you."

It was at that moment that a back door had burst open and the naked redhead ran out.

3

IT IS NO FUN to get your head smacked by the tail of a passing shark. As I mentioned earlier, my head was in no great shakes to begin with, having suffered considerable damage in the hills of Kentucky. Now the shark did his bit by knocking me senseless and scraping off a couple more inches of skin.

I don't know how long I was out. It couldn't have been long, because I must have subconsciously been holding my breath, and it was still in my lungs when Charity hauled me to the surface. She had my chin cupped in one hand as she stroked toward the ladder.

The water around us was frothy and red. I decided that I was bleeding to death. "Don't use a tourniquet," I gasped. "It's hard on the windpipe."

Charity made a gurgling sound that sounded suspiciously like an unladylike curse.

"Let go," I sputtered. "I'm all right."

She went up the ladder ahead of me. The water had plastered her double knit slacks to her like a second skin. But I didn't pause to admire the view. I remembered what

14

the experts had said about bleeding in the water when sharks were around.

My gun was still clenched in my right hand. Water ran from its muzzle.

As I got to the top of the ladder, Charity peered over my shoulder and closed her eyes. She swayed, almost fell. I turned around. What I saw was enough to make *me* close my eyes, too.

The shark was still circling in the center of the pool. Twice, he rolled to the surface and disturbed something floating there.

On the second pass I saw what it was.

Part of a naked, glistening torso swirled in the red-stained water and, slowly, sank.

I pulled down on the shark and squeezed off two rounds. The water spurted in high spouts and the creature dove for the bottom. I couldn't tell if I had hit him or if he'd just been scared off by the noise.

Charity sat down on the pool deck and put her head between her knees. She said, "No . . . no. Not again."

I squeezed the tense muscles at the back of her neck hard enough to make her wince. "Straighten up, baby," I said. "Let's find out what's going on here."

"Yes, what *is* going on here?" said a voice behind me.

I whirled, the pistol ready. Then, feeling foolish, I lowered it.

A handsomely dressed young woman was there, her eyes blinking in the glare of the floodlights. She was on the sunny side of thirty, with long, straight blonde hair.

15

"If you're out for target practice," she said, looking at the gun, "how about plinking beer cans on the beach instead of chipping up my swimming pool? And how did you get over the fence?"

"We drove in the gate," I said. "A lady named Lisa Dantzler invited us to pay a visit."

"I'm Lisa Dantzler," she said. "But I've never seen either of you before."

Charity gripped my arm and stood up. She dripped water on the terrazzo deck. Her voice trembled, but it was strong when she said, "I'm Charity Tucker. This is Ben Shock. An attorney named Conrad phoned my New York office and instructed us to come here."

"Oh," said Lisa Dantzler. She brushed back her blonde hair. "Yes, I'm sorry. I thought I heard the front door, but I was busy and—" She stared down into the water. "What did you shoot at in the pool? It's all red."

"I wouldn't advise you to take a moonlit dip," I said. "There's a shark in there, and I'm afraid he chewed up somebody."

The water was quiet. I tried to see the shark, but the blood and the reflection of the lights made it impossible to look beneath the surface.

Charity began, "She was—"

I cut her off. No point in letting Lisa know how much we had seen. "We got here and the shark was attacking someone. I tried to help and fell in. Then Charity jumped in to pull me out. But somebody else didn't make it. Do you have any idea who it might be?"

16

Lisa Dantzler shook her head. "I haven't seen my maid tonight. But she's not allowed—I mean, she never uses the pool."

As if on cue, the water swirled gently and a limp, still, terribly white hand rose briefly to the surface.

Lisa Dantzler screamed.

Charity moved to Lisa quickly and led her back toward the house. I studied the pool. If the shark was still down there, I wanted to put a .38 slug through his head. For no rational reason. You can't blame a shark for eating whatever's put before him. Clean your swimming pool, little shark, the fishes are starving in Europe. But I was mad. Vengeance isn't a nice word in today's psychology-oriented society, but I ached for a little of it right now. I couldn't erase the picture of that slim, naked body from my mind.

But there wasn't anything to see except a growing winestain of blood that filled the pool from edge to edge.

A door slammed. A heavy male voice said, "What the hell's all the shooting?"

Lisa said something to the tall, husky man who had appeared, and he shaded his eyes from the floodlights and looked toward me. He helped Charity guide Lisa to a chair, and came over to the edge of the pool and stood beside me, staring at the crimson water.

"My God," he said softly.

"Are you Lisa's lawyer?"

He shook his head. "No . . ." He was fascinated by the horror in the pool. I turned away to force him to follow

17

me. "No," he repeated. "I'm her brother-in-law. Nick Wiggins. You must be the investigators she mentioned." He glanced back at the pool. "Christ, what a thing to happen. Who was it?"

Very interesting. How did he know the blood had come from a "who" instead of an "it"? I examined Nick Wiggins. He was fortyish, all muscle fitted neatly into a well-cut sports jacket that hadn't come from Sears.

"Maybe we'd better go inside," I said. "Somebody's going to have to phone the police."

"Police?" cut in Lisa. "We don't want any fuss made—"

"I don't see where you have any choice," I told her. "You can't expect to have a shark kill someone in your swimming pool without attracting a little attention."

"Shark?" said Nick Wiggins. "Lisa, you haven't been fooling with the inlet screen, have you?"

Charity took Lisa Dantzler firmly by the elbow. "Inside," she said. "You don't know who's out there in the darkness right now, listening."

Lisa led the way, with Charity at her side. Nick Wiggins and I followed.

Although this was only the back entrance, the house's interior bore out the grandiose promise made by its exterior. David O. Selznick made a big mistake, building all those sets when this was right here, waiting and ready. Heavy cut-glass chandeliers dangled from the fifteen-foot ceilings. The walls were white stucco, hung with heavy tapestries and covered with original paintings.

"I'll get us a drink," said Nick Wiggins, vanishing toward what must have been the kitchen. When the door swung open, it was like looking into the Houston Astrodome.

"I presume Mr. Wiggins is married to your sister?" Charity said, standing near a walk-in fireplace to avoid dripping on the expensive carpet.

"That's right," said Lisa. "Millie is in Biloxi for the week. We have an estate—a house—there, too." She looked at Charity's soggy hair. "I'm sorry, dear. You'll want to change."

"Good idea," I said. "I'll get our bags."

As I slurped my way toward the front door, I heard Charity say, "Miss Dantzler, you really have to call the police," and Lisa replied, "Must I?" I heard a phone being picked up, and then Lisa said shortly, "Oh, all right, if you're going to force the issue. Give it to me. I know the Chief."

Some lady. A bloody human torso floating in her swimming pool and she doesn't think a fuss ought to be made. . . .

Well, why not, Shock? More and more we form incapsulated little enclaves, barricaded by locks and unlisted phones against the intruding outside. Whatever we were down here to check out, I'd lay nine to five it had something to do with an outsider intruding into Lisa Dantzler's private little chunk of the world. The economists claim the population explosion is over in this country, that our birth rate exactly equals the death rate. In which case, who's moving into all those split-level traps the developers are

19

throwing up in what used to be peaceful countryside?

I opened the Fleetwood's door to reach in for the keys, and then my knees went out from under me and I sank down on the front seat and leaned against the steering wheel. My stomach churned and I had to swallow hard.

Old Man Skull is always out there waiting for you, and when you least expect it, he steps up to tap you on your unwilling shoulder. He had been closer this time than I liked to think about. A savaging of teeth, a release of viscera and torn flesh, the last, unbelieving cry of despair . . . It comes to all of us.

But not just yet. Please.

My knees stopped shaking and I took the key and opened the trunk. My battered B-4 bag was lying on top of the air tanks and the regulator. I took it, and Charity's smaller overnight case, slammed the trunk, and went back inside.

Charity was already warm and dry in a robe borrowed from some offstage closet. A large woman who reminded me of nothing so much as a blue overstuffed chair had Charity's clothes draped over her arm. She saw me dripping my way toward the fireplace and smiled. In rich accents O'Kearny, she said, "Sure, and here's another one. Have we been having a wee spot of Push-Me-in-the-Pool, Miss Lisa?"

"Don't joke, Margaret," said Lisa. "This is serious."

"I'm knowing that," said Margaret. "But if we don't laugh, we cry."

"Margaret will show you your room," Lisa Dantzler

told me. "You can change, and then we'd better talk before the police get here."

"Give me five minutes," I said, handing Charity her suitcase and picking up my drink.

It took closer to three. I eyed the shower longingly, remembering the blood in the water. But that could wait. When I'd said "five minutes," Charity's eyes had met mine and she gave a little shake of her head.

So I hid my gun, wondering how I would explain it to the police if they found a shark with .38 caliber holes in his hide, dried off with a bath towel approximately the size of the average living room rug, and slipped into khaki pants and a sports shirt.

Along the way I finished the bourbon, and took the empty glass down with me.

Nick Wiggins was seated beside his sister-in-law in the living room when I rejoined them. Charity was curled up in a wicker cane chair near the fireplace, which now had a small fire igniting under the obviously skilled hands of Margaret, the maid.

"How long before the police get here?" I asked.

Lisa Dantzler spread her hands. "Not long. Their main office is located downtown."

"Then they ought to be here by now," I said. "Downtown isn't more than five minutes away."

She looked embarrassed. "I—well, I didn't spell out what had happened. I only said that I had to see the Chief on something important when it was convenient."

I slammed my empty glass down on a nearby table.

Nick Wiggins jumped up, grabbed it and headed for a bottle perched on the mantel. "Lady," I said, "you've got a dead body floating around your swimming pool in assorted pieces. Your Chief may be a little peeved when he shows up expecting to soothe you about someone trespassing or swiping watermelons or whatever it is they swipe around here."

"Ben," said Charity, "let's hear what Lisa wants to tell us."

I took the drink Nick offered and sat down in another of the wicker chairs. It made me feel like Sidney Greenstreet in *Casablanca*. But wait a minute, wasn't Greenstreet the crook?

Oh, well. I sighed. "Go ahead," I said.

"My family," began Lisa Dantzler, "has been involved in the oil business for several decades. Principally in Venezuela, although in recent years we have become active in offshore drilling in the Gulf."

"There's a lot of money in oil," I said sagely.

"And a lot of opposition to our manner of drilling," said Nick Wiggins. "Since those blowouts in Santa Barbara, operating an offshore rig is about as popular as strip mining. The ecology freaks ignore the fact that we've invested millions in an attempt to keep this nation independent of foreign energy sources and accuse us of raping the environment and polluting the ocean."

"I've heard the argument," I said. "I even agree with some of it. But so what? I know people who think my Fleetwood is roughly equivalent to the gas chambers at

22

Buchenwald. It's all in how you look at it, and from which side."

"Well, the other side," said Lisa, "has been harassing my company, and my workmen, and *me* for the past six months. We have had public hearings, given speeches, films, demonstrations, proving that our drilling operation is perfectly safe. We will *not* drop the water table, we will *not* pollute the beaches, we will *not* kill the fish or spoil the shrimping. But none of this does any good. Those against us are fanatics. Logic does not enter into it. Reasoning is helpless."

I nodded toward the swimming pool. "Do you think that accident out there could have anything to do with this campaign of harassment?" I didn't mention that I knew the naked redhead had emerged from this house.

Something was wrong here. I could feel it, with the instinct of a cop who senses something *hinkey* about a man who appears to be walking normally down a street. It is a sense you develop, or you don't last on the force. Maybe I had developed it too much, because oddly enough it was that very instinct that led me to too many criminals who resisted, and to too many of my bullets that didn't hit the leg where I'd aimed, but the head where I hadn't. I got the message and resigned before I could be thrown off the Force. In New York's finest, you aren't supposed to hurt the nice crooks.

Lisa and Nick puzzled me. Didn't they *know* there had been a redhead, naked or not, in their house just moments ago? I wouldn't have enjoyed the job, but we should have

23

been out at the pool right now with one of those long-handled skimmers, trying to identify whoever it was laying torn and bloody at its bottom.

And none of this was lost on Charity. But she was intent on pumping Lisa of as much information as possible, so I played along.

Bluntly, Nick Wiggins said, "If there was a shark in the pool, it couldn't have been an accident. That's a salt water pool; it's filled by tidal action through a large conduit. But there's a protective screen to keep out marine life and debris."

"Is the conduit large enough for a shark to work through?" I asked.

"If the screen were removed, yes. But I've never heard of a shark going into one. Tidal pools are common down here on the Gulf. And this is the first shark that's ever been reported in one."

"Nick, please," said Lisa. "We know that nobody drove up with a truck and dumped it there. It *had* to come in from the Gulf."

"Your lawyer," said Charity, "mentioned that this was a simple investigative assignment. He was aware that we do not carry credentials in this state. But what happened in your pool changes things considerably."

"Oh, don't worry about money," Lisa said impatiently. "We have plenty of that and we aren't afraid of spending it. What I want is your assurance before the police get here that you will be working for *me*—for us. I did not expect violence to enter into the case, so naturally your compen-

24

sation will be adjusted." She stared at me defiantly. "Well? Yes or no?"

I shrugged.

Charity said, "Yes. On one condition. We aren't in the business of covering up for murderers. If we find a killer, it doesn't matter which side he's on. We blow the whistle."

"That's fair," said Nick Wiggins. He looked anxiously at his sister-in-law. "What do you say, Lisa? We haven't much time."

She stared at us. "If there are any killers to be found, they won't be on our side." Then, defiantly: "Stay, or go. If you stay, I'll make it worth your while. If you go, you get nothing."

"If we go," Charity said quiety, "we get half of our basic fee plus whatever it costs to clean our clothes."

Nick Wiggins choked with laughter. "Cleaning fees? You're wonderful!"

"We'll stay," I said. "If the accident in the pool has nothing to do with what you hired us for, that's the end of it and the original deal holds. But if we're mixed up with murder, the fee doubles and you pay half of it on the barrelhead."

Lisa spread her hands. "Money," she said, almost sneering. "What's money?"

"Try doing without it and you'll see," I told her.

She started to answer, but the low snarl of a police siren outside silenced her. Whoever was out there had slid up almost behind my car and then just touched the button for a second. I knew that was a signal to others of his crew

25

who might, for all I knew, have the place surrounded.

The door chime pealed.

"Margaret," said Lisa Dantzler, "please answer the door."

Blandly, the maid said, "Are you in, mum?"

"Of course I'm in!" said Lisa. "That's the police."

"As you say," Margaret answered, going to the door. She escorted a uniformed man into the living room. He wore trim khakis, a blue necktie, and a very large revolver.

"It's Chief Gautier," said Margaret. She pronounced it "Go-chay."

"Oh, Ross," said Lisa. "Please come in."

He held his Stetson by its brim. As he came toward her, his eyes flicked around the room. I could tell that he wasn't missing a thing.

"I got your message, Miz Dantzler," he said in a deep southern accent. "And just about that time I had word that there'd been shooting out this way, so I took the liberty of bringing along a couple of my men. They're outside."

"You're so kind," said Lisa. She had turned the full flame of her charm onto Chief Ross Gautier. And it was rolling off his back like water off a duck. He was immune. I felt a surge of admiration for him. I was only getting the fallout of her smile, and it made my stomach sink.

"What seems to be the trouble?" he asked.

"Oh, something dreadful," she said. "Apparently a fish got into our pool and—"

"A fish?" he said softly.

26

"Well, a shark. And according to this gentleman"—this "gentleman" was *me*—"someone apparently fell in and was—" She paused, and Ross Gautier filled the breach: "You mean, ma'am, hurt? Or worse?"

"Much worse," she said. "It's absolutely horrible. Blood all over. We'll have to get the pool drained and scrubbed out, of course."

"Who was it?"

"I don't know."

He looked at me. "You're?"

"Ben Shock. This is Charity Tucker. I don't know who it was either. We'd just arrived and when I heard the commotion, I tried to help. But it didn't do any good."

"Was it you that did all the shooting?"

"Yes." Hoist on my own illegal pistol. I wondered what they did to people in Mississippi for having unregistered firearms.

He saw the uncertainty on my face.

"Where you from, Mr. Shock?"

"Well, you might say New York."

"Your gun registered up there?"

"Uh . . . not any more. And we just got here—"

He held up his hand. "Don't worry about it, as long as you weren't carrying it concealed. Or until we find bullet holes in whoever's out there in Miz Dantzler's pool."

He looked toward the back door. "Maybe I'd better go out and get my men organized," he said to Lisa. "Mr. Shock, you want to come with me?"

"Any time," I said, meaning it. Ross Gautier was the

27

kind of cop I liked—straight, serious, hard as nails, and most of all, fair.

As we went through the door, he spoke quietly in a voice that would not have carried three feet, "You're not operating without a license, are you, Shock?"

"Perish the thought," I told him. "My partner and I—"

"Partner? That cute blonde?"

"That cute blonde," I said, "knows more about the law than you and me and Perry Mason all put together."

"You didn't answer me."

"No," I said. "We're not doing any P.I., if that is what you mean by operating. But we *are* trouble-shooters, and Miss Dantzler called us in to see if we can help out with some problems she's having with her offshore oil operation."

"No law against that," said Gautier. "But while you're shooting those troubles, don't let me hear of you telling anyone you're a private investigator, or even implying it. Understood?"

"Chief," I said, "I read you loud and clear."

We reached the pool. He peered over into the murky red of the water.

"I don't see any shark," he said.

"Maybe he's laying on the bottom," I said. "I threw three shots at him. Or maybe he got out the way he got in."

"What really happened here, Shock?"

I told him. How we'd arrived, come around to the back.

28

And, for the first time, I spoke of the naked redhead. He frowned.

"Redhead, Ben?"

So now it was Ben. Obviously I had become one of the good guys. That was a step forward.

"A carrot-top. And it was real, too. Remember, she was naked."

Ross Gautier waved one of the uniformed troopers over. "Call Jackson," he said. "Tell them we've got a probable homicide down here and it's a hot one. Get the MBI on the stick. We need their forensic specialists immediately if not sooner."

"Right, Chief," said the trooper, taking off toward his squad car.

"What's the MBI?" I asked.

"Mississippi Bureau of Investigation," he said. It figured. Hear MBI in Singing River, Mississippi, and what have you got? Gautier grinned at me. "We have a few experts down here—men who have been with Hoover and even the New York State CID."

"I'm impressed. What can I do to help?"

"Does your job with Miss Dantzler have anything to do with what happened here?"

"I hope not," I said honestly. "I'm up to my ears in killings. I hope this was just a lousy accident. Listen, Chief, let me save you some time. You're going to want to check me out. Call Captain Murphy on the NYPD. He was my boss until a month or so ago. And check Chief

29

Miles Cook up in Pilgrim's Pride, Massachusetts. He and I had a little problem to solve together back in July."

Gautier didn't fool around. He wrote down the names and nodded. "Thanks, Ben. That *will* save time, and the sooner I can stop watching you, the sooner you get down to work."

"That's what I figured," I said. "Ross—" I looked at him as I said his first name, and he nodded. "Why did you give me that look when I told you she was a redhead?"

"I better not say until I'm sure," he said. "But as soon as I know, I'll tell you."

"As soon as you know about her? Or me?"

He gave me a tight smile.

"Both of you."

4

LISA DANTZLER gave Charity and me a couple more drinks, suggested supper, got refused. Nick Wiggins had slumped into one corner as if he were set for the night. Charity still wore the borrowed robe, and she looked kittenish and cute in it.

I made yawning gestures for a while and finally Charity took the hint and excused herself and went upstairs. I hung around for one more drink. Nick made this one.

"Are you in the oil business, too?" I asked.

"In a way," he said, smiling thinly. "Oil is like any other natural resource. It's where you find it."

Over his shoulder, I saw a framed wedding picture. Nick was the groom, in a full-dress outfit complete with striped morning pants. The girl on his arm resembled Lisa slightly. The picture was in color, and the girl was a flaming redhead. I tried to remember the one in the pool, but her face kept getting mixed up with the dorsal fin of the shark, and I couldn't bring the image into focus.

Nick noticed my gaze and turned. He picked up the

31

photograph and held it out to me. "That's Millie," he said. "Isn't she beautiful?"

"Lovely," I agreed.

"Too beautiful for me," he said, slugging away at his drink. "I don't deserve her."

I realized that he was further along than I'd thought. On the one hand, I wanted to pump him now that his guard was down. But I liked him. It would be unsporting to take advantage of his temporary weakness.

So who said I was a sportsman? I dug in.

"Do you both live in Biloxi, Nick?"

"Sometimes. I—travel a good deal, Ben. Too much." He finished off his drink. "But you can't make sales unless you make the calls, right?"

"Right," I said. "Want me to freshen that?"

Coldly, Lisa said, "Nick has had enough."

He stared at her. "Not nearly enough," he said. "Thanks, Ben. Straight up, if you please. I don't like the taste of the water around here. Among other things."

As I made his drink, Lisa said, "How nice, Nick, that you've found someone else to fetch and carry for you."

Outside, a light flared. At first I thought it was lightning, a forerunner of the storm that must surely be coming. But when it did not fade, I realized that Chief Gautier and his men must have brought in some powerful floodlights of their own.

I handed Nick the glass. He nodded his thanks.

Lisa said, "You must be very tired, Mr. Shock."

How broad a hint do you need?

"Bushed," I said. "You'll forgive me?"

She smiled slowly. "You're forgiven," she said. "We'll talk in the morning."

As I went upstairs, I glanced back at Nick Wiggins. He was leaning against the mantel with the dazed look of a man who has been sapped in the back of the head with a sockful of nickels. Lisa Dantzler sat across from him, alert and aware of every motion, every *thought,* in the room.

Mounting the stairs, I thought, I do not like thee, Lisa D; the reason why I cannot see; but this I know, and know for free; I do not like thee, Lisa D.

Apologies to Lewis Carroll, or whoever wrote the original.

The door to my room was open and the light streamed out into the darkened hallway. I went in and shut the door. The shower invited, and I accepted. And the water ran red at my feet.

It sickened me. Who needs blood running down his shins? Why the hell wasn't I sitting in my little Starcraft jigging for walleyes on Lake Oneida and drinking cold Utica Club? I hadn't tried any Jax yet, but how could it ever be as good? I turned down the hot faucet and let the cold water tighten my chest and gasp my breathing.

Then I danced out and had at my dripping hide with another of the room-sized towels. I hadn't unpacked my robe yet, so I strolled into the bedroom with the towel draped over my neck and everything else hanging out.

33

Naturally, Charity was sitting there.

I tried to get the towel down into a decent position. Instead, it fell on the floor.

"You might knock," I said.

She smiled and flicked off the bedside lamp, but now at least I could get the robe out of my B-4 bag without feeling a total idiot. I have never been a big one for the nudist scene, even with one who is as close as Charity. It isn't modesty—more likely, it is an awareness that I do not have the fancy muscles and nice tan and the rest that the Hollywood beefcake boys splash all over centerfolds these days. I need all the help I can get, and that includes candlelight and soft music.

"Your virtue is safe, Ben," she said. "I just wanted to talk."

I might have ventured a sharp rejoinder. In the months we have spent together, talk is just about all Charity and I have been able to manage. It's nobody's fault. By her own admission, she was once a normally lusty and enjoying bedmate. But the occasion of our meeting was one not calculated to raise passion between us. I was on duty in Riverside Park and found her under the squirming body of a rapist. He made the mistake of pulling a gun and I splattered his brains. All over Charity Tucker. Since then, that bastard's twitching carcass has always been between us.

"You've acquired a nice one for us this time," I said.

Charity touched my head. "Your hair's wet."

I let her keep her hand there. I am like Old Blue, the

hound we'd met up in Kentucky. I like having my head stroked.

But I was not willing to overlook what seemed to be shaping up into a very bad assignment. "Baby, why did we have to take on this can of worms? I don't know who that poor girl is out there in the pool, or what connection she has with Lisa D., but if what we saw wasn't murder, it was damned close to it. Did you see her eyes? She was stoned out of her mind with liquor or drugs or both."

I got up and went to the window. Down at the pool I could see khaki-clad men with nets dipping terrible *things* from the wine-colored water. I closed the shutters. The room got dark.

Charity moved beside me. "Did you see the old man, Ben?"

"What old man?"

"In the bedroom at the end of the hall. The door was partly open when I came up. He was sitting up in bed, just staring out into the night."

"So Lisa's got a grandpa who sits in bed staring into the night. What's so unusual about that?"

"I don't know." Her hands kneaded the muscles in my shoulders. The thumbs bit in and made me gasp. "You're tense."

"Wrestling with sharks does that to me."

"Lie down."

I stretched out on the bed. She unknotted the robe and slipped it away from my body. Her hands were strong and probing against my tight muscles.

35

"Ben?"

"What, baby?"

"I was so afraid for you."

"Me too," I said.

Something wet hit my spine. It wasn't sweat. She was crying.

"You were almost killed."

"Somebody jumped in and saved me. For which, many thanks."

"I didn't even think. The shark hit you, and you went under, and the next thing I knew I was in the water. If he'd come after you again, I think I would have bitten him back."

I smiled in the darkness. "I think you would have, too. You're some woman, blondie."

She slapped my rump. "Don't call me that!"

"Are you trying to tell me, after all we've been through together, that you're not a natural blonde?"

Her hands resumed their massage. "I just don't like it when you call me names you must have used on—" she breathed in a ragged sigh—"on your other women."

"Of which there were many."

She slapped me again, more gently this time. "How many?"

"Thousands."

"How many?"

"Serious ones? Two. You and one other."

She kneaded the stiffness out of my deltoids. Then: "Who was she?"

"Would you believe, a social worker."

She laughed. "I'd believe that, knowing you. What happened?"

"She never would listen to me, or my pop—he was a sergeant in the precinct where she worked. We told her never, *never* trust a junkie. But with Amanda—"

"That was her name? Amanda?"

"That was her name. With her, it was enough if you were in trouble. She was on your side a thousand percent. She had it all worked out. It was the People against the Establishment. The People were good, and the Establishment was bad."

"Where did that put you?"

"Right in the middle. It was rough. I think it might have worked itself out. But the Beautiful People didn't give us time. Three of them caught her in a tenement hallway, dragged her up to the roof and raped her for a couple of hours before throwing her down the air shaft. She'd been on her way to visit one of her cases, a junkie who lived on the top floor. He heard what was going on, but he was afraid to come out and use the hall phone to call for help."

Charity eased herself down on the bed beside me. "And that's part of the reason why you're such a hard-nose?"

I thought about what she said. Well, why not? A man isn't born full-shaped. Amanda's senseless death *had* helped harden me into whatever I'd become. "Yes," I said. "Baby, my old man was one of the best cops I knew. He didn't coddle the punks. If he caught them swiping hub-

37

caps or busting open gum machines, he applied the point of his nightstick where it did the most good. Justice was instant and sure. That was before the headline-hunting lawyers and bleeding-heart do-gooders appeared on the scene. We were hungry in those days. When you're hungry, you don't have time to go around sticking up for the rights of the oppressed. You're too busy being oppressed yourself to look out for anyone else. Maybe a few micks or wops got clobbered by mistake. Maybe even a nigger or two."

"Ben!"

"Cool it, baby. Those were the names we used. I was a mick. That's what my own pop called me. Of course, if a wop ever called me mick, we'd probably have us a little knuckledusting. What the hell, they were only labels to pin on us. Anyway, a few of the innocent probably got swept up along with the guilty. But what was the penalty? A lump on the shin that went away in a few days. We didn't get a chance to graduate to nice things like mugging and rape and murder, because except for a very few hard cases, we were shown the error of our ways and given a chance to repent without picking up criminal records to dog us the rest of our lives." I sat up. "Where the hell are my cigarettes?"

"They're all wet."

I mumbled a little and lay back. Her hand traced tiny circles on my chest. "Keep doing that, lady," I warned, "and we might have a little job of rape here, too."

"Oh, promises, promises," she said.

Her voice was gentle, and I felt a stirring in the pit of my stomach. If only it could work between us . . .

I forced myself to go on. "Today, what happens? Kids pick up rap sheets with ten, fifteen, twenty arrests by the time they're eighteen. Why? Because nobody cracked down on them that first time, when they still had a choice. There's two ways of getting smart, baby. You can get book-smart, and you can get street-smart. Our kids today are street-smart. They know how overcrowded the courts are. They know their *rights*. Never mind about the rights of the victims. They know how slim the chances are of even being caught, because nobody wants to get involved."

"Amanda got involved," Charity said.

"The wrong way! She saw them as victims, not as victimizers."

She pressed herself against me. "But, Ben, isn't there some truth in both?"

Angrily, I said, "Of course there is! That's what makes it so hard. Listen, how the hell did we get on this?"

"You were talking about Amanda."

"Screw Amanda!" I said savagely. "She was stupid and now she's dead and she deserved it!"

I turned over. Charity stroked my forehead.

"Shhh," she said softly. "Shhh."

39

5

Dawn arrived with a screeching of sea gulls and a dull, leaden light that oozed through the shutters.

Charity must have opened them when she left, somewhere in the anxious hours that come after midnight.

We had tried, and it was no good. That night in Riverside Park still held us in its murky grasp.

"You'd better give up on me, Ben," she said, trembling in my arms. "It's never going to work."

Then it was my turn to whisper "Shhh . . ."

She kissed me when she left, and I lay there alone, drifting into sleep.

During the night, I came awake once, battling the shark again. I had drenched the sheets with sweat. I got up and took the flask of J. T. S. Brown out of the B-4 bag and gulped down a burning mouthful. It calmed the bare nerve-ends, and I was able to slip into a dreamless void that lasted until the sea gulls called reveille.

I slipped on a pair of loud boxer shorts and went over to look out the window.

The sky had a puffy, gray cast. The Gulf of Mexico was

flat and turgid. It looked more like heavy burned grease than water. The air was oppressive and close.

Down around the circular swimming pool, a silent ring of men stood. Some wore uniforms, some were in plain clothes. Probably the MBI forensic specialists. They were watching water drain out of the pool. Gravity was being helped along by a little put-put engine that drove a pump connected to a long hose. It was spurting water against a row of stunted pine trees.

There was no sign of the shark.

The water was down to a foot or so in depth. Things floated in it. I hoped they weren't what I thought they were.

I finished dressing and went down. My beard itched against my neck. Shaving could wait until later.

Chief Ross Gautier was standing near the pool with a mug of coffee in his hand. He looked haggard and weary.

"Good morning, Ben. Coffee?"

He nodded toward an urn. I said, "Thanks," and helped myself. "How's it going?"

"Lousy. Two of my men tossed their cookies, and I don't blame them a bit. Jesus, but a shark does awful things. He didn't just bite that poor girl—he *shredded* her."

The chief inclined his head toward a canvas-covered shape that lay on the pool deck.

"Any sign of the shark?" I asked.

"No. He must have come in the conduit, and he went out the same way." Ross Gautier scowled. "If you're going to pack a gun, I wish you'd learn to use it. No sign that you hit him."

"It's tricky, shooting into the water," I said.

"I know. I'm sorry, Ben. I'm just wore out. Oh, Captain Murphy says hello. And he wanted me to tell you that the governor of New York just proposed the death penalty for dope pushers. He said that might bring a smile."

I shrugged. "I guess I was just ahead of my time. I take it I'm cleared."

"All the way. Like I said, don't give anybody the idea you're a P.I., but other than that, take your best hold."

"Thanks. Have you seen Miss Dantzler?"

"No," he said tightly. "But I will. Oh, yes, you better believe I will."

I looked at the canvas-covered bundle. "Did you find out who she was?"

He didn't answer. "How do you figure these rich people?" he said. "A beautiful white sand beach out there, and the whole Gulf of Mexico to swim in, and they go and dig a swimming pool—and instead of filling it with fresh water, which I could maybe understand, they dig a tunnel so they can use salt water right out of the Gulf. Ben, am I backward? That just doesn't make sense."

"How do they get the salt water in?" I asked.

He nodded toward the conduit, which was almost completely above the present water line. "The pool's dug lower than the high-tide level. When the tide comes in, it floods the pool through that conduit. Then they close a floodgate

42

and it holds the water back. When they want to change the water, they open the gate at low tide. That's what we did this morning. But we're helping it along with that pump."

I saw that a net had been stretched across the wide mouth of the big conduit. Gautier noticed and said, "That's to catch anything that might be floating in the water. He—he tore her up pretty bad."

That cold hand brushed my shoulder again. He had nearly torn me up, too.

"Who was she?" I repeated.

Gautier walked slowly over to the canvas and lifted it. She stared up at me. Her face was white—white as chalk. It made her hair look even brighter red. Her lips were slightly parted, as if she were trying to force a smile.

"Know her?" asked Ross Gautier.

I didn't have to think. Now that the effects of the fear and the liquor had worn off, I could remember.

"Yes," I said. "I saw her photograph last night."

"In there?" Gautier jerked his head toward the big house. I nodded. "Yeah," he went on. "That's why I got me a few questions to ask around here. That's Miss Millie, all right. Now, I heard she was staying up in Biloxi. So what is she doing running around naked and jumping into a swimming pool full of sharks?"

"Good question. Ross—she looked kind of spaced out to me. As if she were high on something."

"I don't doubt that," said Gautier. "We've had stories

about Miss Lisa and some of her friends."

I finished my coffee. "I thought you and she were old buddies."

"Her and me?" He gave a harsh laugh. "Don't you ever say that downtown, boy. As far as Lisa Dantzler is concerned, I'm the head of her private security force. She pays me about as much mind as she does anybody else who works for her, and my guess is, you've already had a taste of that yourself."

Remembering her cold dismissal of Charity and me the previous night, I said, "Just an appetizer."

"Well," said Gautier, "I'm sure sorry this happened to Miss Millie. But I don't lose any sleep over Lisa Dantzler."

He was coming on so strong, I wondered . . .

6

THE BREAKFAST TABLE was laid, but nobody was eating. Charity was sipping coffee and talking quietly with Lisa Dantzler. There was a stranger at the table with them—a slim, bearded man in a bright plaid shirt and heavy canvas trousers. Around his waist was a pistol belt and, in its holster, a .44 caliber Ruger Blackhawk. Heavy artillery. That .44 bullet can knock down a moose—and I know hunters who have done it.

I glanced at Ross Gautier, who gave me a weak grin. "No law against carrying a pistol down here," he said. "Not so long as it ain't concealed." He gave the bearded man a curt nod. "How do, Grover."

"Morning, Chief."

"Ben Shock," said Lisa Dantzler, "meet Grover Ellis. Grover's in charge of Offshore Two, our rig out in the Gulf."

"Mr. Shock," said Grover, sticking out his hand. He was skinny, but he had a grip. I gave him back just a little more than he offered, and he winced. He kept his eyes fixed on mine, though, and I thought I saw the slightest

45

suggestion of a humorous wink.

"Where's Mr. Wiggins?" asked the Chief.

"Still sleeping," said Lisa. "Is it important?"

Bluntly, Gautier said, "I reckon it might be. That's his wife dead out there in the pool."

All right, he really *didn't* like her. I've never seen tragic news presented so bluntly.

Lisa stared at him. "What?" she said numbly.

"That's Millie Wiggins out there," said Gautier, watching her carefully.

Lisa still stared. Her lips opened noiselessly. She cleared her throat. "My sister?" she said softly.

"No doubt about it," he said.

"Millie?" she said in a tiny voice.

"Dead as a doornail."

She started to move toward the door and then went down in a heap. I've seen many fake faints. This wasn't one of them. Her head made a solid clunk when she hit the floor.

Charity got up and gave Ross Gautier a solid slap across the cheek. He staggered back, his face flushing violent red.

"You bastard!" said my girl.

He rubbed his hand against his face, chewing on his lip. "Sorry," he said shortly. "I know what that must have looked like to strangers. But I had my reasons." He turned and headed for the door. There, he looked back and said, "Grover, I don't have to remind you to keep that there pistol in plain sight at all times."

46

"That's the way I like it, Chief," said Grover Ellis. He watched Gautier leave, then spat deliberately on the floor. "Cracker son of a bitch. He'll get his."

Charity had knelt near Lisa. "Hand me some water," she said.

I gave her a glass. She sprinkled some of it on the fallen girl's forehead. Lisa's eyes opened. She looked around.

"I must have slipped," she said.

"Just be quiet," said Charity. "You had a bad shock."

Lisa sat up. "Nick," she said. "My God, *Nick.*" She looked around in sudden fright. "Who will tell him?"

"Don't worry about that now," I said. "Where did you hide the booze? You could use a shot."

"Not in the morning," she said.

"Don't argue."

She closed her eyes. "In the kitchen."

I went into the Astrodome. Margaret was cooking something on the stove. She turned.

"Lisa needs you," I said.

She made no sound, just headed for the door with a swift, quiet purpose.

I poured a hefty shot of bourbon and went back into the dining room.

Margaret and Charity were helping Lisa into a chair. Grover Ellis still sat in the chair where he had been ever since Lisa had fainted. Suddenly I shared Gautier's dislike for him.

"Don't bust your back," I said.

47

He smiled up at me lazily. "I'm just hired help," he said. "I know better than to put my dirty hands on the boss lady."

He crossed his legs and folded his arms over his chest.

I kicked one foot and his legs went out from under him and he fell out of the chair. His hand flicked to the revolver butt, and I got ready to kick him between the eyes. Then he relaxed. But I didn't.

"How does it feel down there?" I said.

"Cool," he said. "Had your fun, city boy? Is it all right if I get up now? I wouldn't want to be sucker-punched."

"Both of you, stop it!" said Lisa. "Don't we have enough trouble?"

"He kicked me," said Grover Ellis.

"Shut up." Lisa turned to Margaret. "Ask Mr. Wiggins to come down, Margaret. It's important."

Margaret hesitated. She looked at me.

"Need help?" I asked

"Oh, all right," said Lisa. Then, to Charity, "Why is it that every unattractive, unmarried, unwanted woman supposes she'll be instantly raped if she goes into a man's bedroom?"

Smiling at me, Charity said, "I suppose it depends on the man."

I stared back. It wasn't very funny. Was that what she wanted? Was I supposed to repeat that moment in time for her, that instant in Riverside Park when her world changed forever?

48

"Come on," I said to Margaret. "I'll ride shotgun for you."

"If you're going," said Lisa, "Margaret can return to the kitchen. You aren't both needed."

Calmly, Margaret said, "And how many will there be for lunch, mum?"

"I'll let you know later," Lisa snapped.

"Very good," said the maid. She strolled back into the kitchen.

I went upstairs to wake Nick Wiggins. That is often my role. When bad news is to be carried, enlist Ben Shock.

The door at the end of the hall was open. I glanced in. Charity had been right. There was an old man in there. He was asleep, snoring gently. Remember the riddle that drove Bernard Shaw mad? When you sleep, is your beard in or out?

It was out.

By the process of elimination and gentle tapping on two unresponsive doors, I found Nick's room. When I rapped, a voice grumbled back, "I'm getting up."

That was good enough. I could return to the dining room, my mission accomplished. Let somebody else do the dirty work.

Instead, I went to my own room, got the J. T. S. Brown and returned. I tapped again and went in.

Nick Wiggins had been lying. He wasn't getting up. He hadn't even gone to bed. He was sprawled across it, fully clothed, dying of a bad case of Gilbey's Disease.

49

"We need a drink," I told him.

I poured two into glasses I found in the bathroom. We clinked them. He winced at the sound.

"You're Ben Shock," he said. I nodded, and he seemed delighted to remember that much of the previous evening. Then he remembered a little more and sat up sharply. The motion obviously disturbed his shaky hold on equilibrium, and he groaned and applied himself to the J. T. S. Brown.

"Feeling better?" I asked after a while.

"No," he said. "Have the police gone?"

I shook my head. "They want to talk to you when you come down."

He fixed hazy eyes in my direction. "Why me?"

"There's bad news."

He lifted the glass slowly and sucked at it.

I said, "Nick—"

"No," he mumbled. He finished the bourbon. Then he examined the glass as if it were Yorick's skull. "Don't tell me."

"But—"

"I said don't tell me. You don't have to. I know. You don't have to say it. I know. It's Millie." He handed me the empty glass. I gave him mine, which was still half filled. He drained it, too, and this time he made the old gesture of throwing it into the fireplace, except there wasn't any fireplace, so it went into the closet. "I think I must have known from the beginning. But I wouldn't let it be. I shut it out. I told you, I didn't deserve her. So they took her away from me."

50

"Who, Nick? Who took her?"

"Who?" He stared at me. He'd lost his train of thought. He was still drunk. He hadn't sobered up during what remained of the night, and the booze I'd just given him hadn't helped.

I went into the bathroom. There wasn't any salt, which would have been best, but there *was* a tube of Alka-Seltzer tablets. I put six of them into a glass of water. What they call a massive overdose. The only dangerous drug in them, though, was aspirin, and a triple dose shouldn't be harmful. I waited until the massive fizzing died down and took the glass back to Nick Wiggins. "Drink this," I said. "All the way."

He made a face, but he drained the glass. Then he sat for a moment as the brew worked its way through his plumbing. I shuddered to think of what was happening down there, as the massive dose of antacids mingled with the stygian pools of his booze-laden stomach. The result was instant and dramatic.

Nick made a lunge for the bathroom. He made it. Then a torrent of undigested food, unassimilated liquor, and assorted noxious fluids burst forth. He leaned over, his head in the bathtub, and gave up everything.

When he'd finished heaving, I said, "Get in the shower."

He mumbled something, so I helped him in with a foot shoved against his posterior, and turned on the cold water. I closed the curtain and yelled, "Get dressed and come on down as soon as you can."

As I left, he called after me, "Thanks, you no-good goddamned son of a bitch!"

"Bloody Mary?" I called back.

"No. Tea."

"We'll have it."

There was a pause. Then: "Thanks, Ben. I mean it."

"Any time," I said.

The old man was still snoring as I went past the open door. He looked happy. I hoped he wasn't Millie Wiggins' grandfather. Enough people were unhappy already.

Downstairs, I found the breakfast table much the same as I had left it. Charity was talking with Grover Ellis.

"We didn't have it like this in Texas City," he said. "Where the hell do these nuts come from? We're putting money in their pockets, meat on their tables. They understand that in Texas. What the hell's wrong with Mississippi?"

I sat down and Margaret brought me a cup of coffee. Have I told you about my war with the coffee bean? It is a noble creation, capable of pure magic and absolute ecstasy in the cup when properly prepared.

My father made the only cup of coffee I have ever been able to enjoy. I do not know exactly how he did it. He was always going to explain, but he never got around to it, and the secret died with him. Since then, like Diogenes, I have wandered with my percolator held high, searching for a cup of honest coffee, and seldom have I found it.

Margaret, alas, did not have the touch. Her brew was acceptable, far above the abomination served in restaurants, but still lacking in that ultimate flavor.

Charity, who knows of my affliction, smiled her condolences.

"What exactly has happened?" I asked.

Grover Ellis scowled at me. "Miss Lisa told me I'm supposed to cooperate with you. I don't know what we're doing wrong—"

"Probably nothing," I said. "We're here to help you, not compete with you."

Maybe the words were too big for him. He didn't take the olive branch.

"Me and my boys can handle whatever they throw," he said. "We don't need any New York muscle."

"Perhaps not," said Charity. "But I think you could use some New York brains."

He glared at her. "Listen, ma'am—"

She went on: "You say that since you arrived in Singing River, your men have been jumped and beaten up when they come ashore. Their drinks are drugged, they're pushed into fights, your cars and trucks are vandalized."

"Sugar in the gas tanks and slashed tires," he said.

"Can't the police do anything?" I asked.

"Those crackers? Bust their own? Don't make me laugh, Shock!"

"That's not the way I read Chief Gautier," I said. "Are you telling me he's looking the other way?"

Ellis hesitated, then backed down. "No," he admitted, "I don't get along with that redneck, but nobody'd ever say he's on the take. Okay, he's honest. What good does that do my guys? They're still getting it in the neck."

"From who?"

He grinned at me. "That's what you've been hired to find out, ain't it? You tell me. I'll bust their asses."

"Don't try it," said Ross Gautier, entering from the pool door. "Ben, you're a stranger here. I don't know how things work where you come from, but anybody who tries busting asses around Singing River will find his own in a sling."

"It's the same all over," I said. "Don't worry, Ross. This isn't the showdown at the O.K. Corral."

"This isn't going to be nice," he said, looking back and forth between me and Lisa Dantzler. "But someone's going to have to identify the—deceased."

"Say it," Lisa told him. "You want me to look at my sister."

Gautier hesitated. "Her husband can do it."

She stood. "No. It's better I do."

Starting for the door, Ross Gautier said, "You too, Ben. You're the only one who saw it happen."

"I saw, too," Charity said.

I waved her down. "You stay here," I said. "Nick may come down. We don't want him out there."

Grover laughed. "A cop with a heart of gold?"

I turned. "You want to be down on the floor again, loudmouth?"

He smiled. "Not just now."

Ross grabbed my arm. "Come on. He's just hotdogging you. You know how it is with those little guys. They've

54

got to come on stronger than anyone else in the world."

"Same to you, Chief," said Grover Ellis.

The pool was completely dry. There were little clumps of weed and broken stone on its bottom. Two policemen were carefully examining the net and removing tiny particles from its mesh. I didn't want to look too closely at what they were.

We stood over the canvas-covered shape. Ross Gautier drew the cloth back enough to uncover the head.

Lisa Dantzler stared down at the still face, at the bloodless lips, at the wide, staring eyes and the tangled mass of red hair.

"Show me more," she said.

"Is that Millie?" asked Ross Gautier.

"Uncover her."

"That isn't necessary," Gautier said.

"You heard me. If you want an identification, do what I said."

"Please."

"*Do it!*"

Silently, he peeled the canvas back.

I don't know what Lisa did. I nearly puked.

The shark had savaged the poor body beneath us. One breast was completely gone, with shreds of flesh and bone extruding from the horrid cavity where the shark had bitten deep. Another scallop had been torn from the inner thigh of her left leg, showing white bone beneath the almost colorless flesh.

"Thank you," said Lisa Dantzler.

Ross Gautier covered the body.

"I don't know why you thought you had to do that, Miz Dantzler," he said.

"Chief," she said, "I don't believe in hiding from reality. I don't know who did this to my sister. But I can assure you, now that I've seen what he—or she—did, I will never forget."

I could agree with that. I'd never forget, either.

"Then you identify this as your sister, Millicent Wiggins, née Dantzler?" said Gautier.

"Come on, Ross," she said. "We both know it's her."

"I know," he said. "It's just the legal form."

"Well, fill it out and I'll sign it," she said. "What happens next?"

"Well," he said slowly, "there ought to be an autopsy."

"Why?" she snapped. "To prove Millie bled to death?"

"To find out what she'd been taking, or drinking, before she fell in that pool."

"You don't leave a thing, do you?"

"I'm sorry," he said. "You must know that I don't have any choice."

"Go ahead. Do it all. When can we have her?"

"Well," he said thoughtfully, "we can get the coroner to come right over from Gulfport. This evening?"

"No later," she said. Then, to me, "Come on, Ben. We've got work to do."

7

NICK WIGGINS sat near the fireplace, a glass of brandy in his hand. His face was dazed. I felt so sorry for the poor bastard that I missed what Lisa Dantzler had just said.

"Mr. Shock!" she snapped. "Pay attention. I was describing the series of sabotage incidents we've been having out on Offshore Two. Have you heard any of it?"

"*I* have," said Charity. "Let's not waste time proving who is boss. What do you have in mind?"

"Grover came in from the tower last night on business," Lisa answered. "That was before the—accident—in the pool. I had planned for him to consult with you this morning. Now I believe the situation is more urgent. Whoever killed my sister is only beginning. And I doubt that we can count on much protection from Chief Gautier and his deputies."

"I asked," Charity repeated, "what you had in mind."

"I think you ought to go out to Offshore Two and have a look around for yourselves. It's another world. I can't describe it to anyone who hasn't been there. You may see something, as outsiders, that we can't because we're too close."

"Good idea," said Charity. "Why are you so defensive about it?"

From his perch near the fireplace, Nick Wiggins mumbled, "Because she's guilty. I've pleaded with her to seek help before now, and she always replied that the Dantzlers spent fifty years ramrodding oil developments through South America without calling for help, and they weren't going to start. But now a Dantzler has been killed, and the name of the game has changed."

"Shut up," said Lisa. "You're disgusting. It's not nine A.M. yet, and you're drunk already."

"Drunk *still,*" said Nick. "I haven't sobered up yet from last night."

"Well, if you can't contribute, shut up."

"I contributed a wife," he said. "What else do you want?"

She focused on her cup of coffee and, to me, said slowly, "A helicopter is on its way over from Gulfport. It will ferry you out to the Texas Tower and wait for your return. I want you to hurry, because this storm is moving in on us."

Quietly, I said, "Let's get one thing straight. Are we required to act on what we discover, or merely pass it along to you?"

"Pass it along. We can take care of our own problems."

"Suppose we can't spare the time? Sometimes discovery

and action are tied together."

"I don't think we'd quibble," Lisa Dantzler said. "The idea is to stop the harassment. I don't care who actually pushes the button."

"Ben," said Nick Wiggins. "Listen. If you find out who caused—what happened to Millie, don't push the button. Find me. I'll do it. Find me, or I'll kill you."

"What the hell is this, Threat City?" I snapped. "Every time we turn around, somebody's threatening something. Listen, Miss Dantzler, I appreciate your desire to suck oil out of the Gulf and make a quick buck. That's the good old American free enterprise system. But I think you're going up against a Sherman tank with nothing but a pistol. You need all the help you can get. Charity and I may cost you more than money—we can cost you time, and that's what you can't afford. Why don't you bring in the big guns? This sounds like a conspiracy, and I think there's a murder, too, so I suggest you spend a dime and call the FBI—"

"No one can purchase courage," she said calmly. "If you're afraid to attempt this assignment, nothing can persuade you."

"Why are you afraid to get this out in the open?"

"That, Mr. Shock, is neither true nor any of your business. You are an employee. Do your job or leave."

I got up. "That's clear enough."

"Sit down, Ben," said Charity. "Miss Dantzler is only shooting off her mouth."

59

"What!" sputtered Lisa.

"Everyone, shut up!" said my girl. "Lisa, I think you owe Ben an apology."

Lisa glared. "I apologize."

I smiled. "I accept."

"Now, Ben? Your turn."

"Me?!"

"You've got better manners than to lay something out like that, even if it is the truth."

I mumbled, "Sorry."

"Also accepted," said Lisa Dantzler.

"Now," said Charity. "Suppose we get down to work?"

"Very well," said Lisa. "The helicopter should be here in a few minutes. It will take you to Offshore Two. Grover will accompany you. You will have carte blanche. Go anywhere on the tower, ask anything, open all locks. Nothing is off limits. I don't care how many feathers you ruffle. But come back with an answer." She turned her head toward the pool, then looked directly at Nick Wiggins. "This has gone far enough."

"Fair," I said. "Grover, I want some information."

"What?"

"Do I have to carry my pistol in a holster?"

"It has to be visible," he said. "You can stick it in your belt, but it better not slip under your coat."

I used to have a nifty little clip-on holster when I was on the Force. But, in a fit of pique when I'd resigned, I cut it up and used the leather to make pads to keep my

60

Mercury outboard motor from digging holes in my Starcraft's transom. Now I would have to poke the .38 down my belt like a South American gunsel. But I was damned if I was going to any offshore drilling tower without it.

Ross Gautier, who had come in without my hearing him, said, "You can borrow one of my shoulder rigs, Ben. But don't wear a coat over it."

Hopefully, I said, "Maybe I could get a permit?"

He shook his head. "You're not by any stretch of the imagination a Mississippi resident."

Gautier turned to a deputy who had entered with him. "Get that shoulder harness out of my trunk. The keys are in the ignition."

"Thanks," I said

"You aren't very well-equipped," smiled the Chief.

"You wouldn't believe this," I said, "but where I live, they frown on honest citizens packing guns. The only ones allowed to do it are the criminals."

He smiled. "I heard all about it," he said. "What do you expect, with nine million city people telling the rest of the state how to live?"

"You," I said, "are anti–Fun City."

"All the way," he said. "I went up there last year for a lab session in check forgery. One night, leaving the hotel, a nigger tried to mug me. I beat the shit out of him."

"What happened?"

"With my accent? Two of his buddies swore I'd tried to push him off the sidewalk and the judge let me out with a fifty-dollar fine and a warning."

"Now," Charity said softly, "if you'd only been a mick . . ."

He scowled. "None of this talk gets us anywhere. Ben, I heard you're going out to that Texas Tower."

"By chopper, if they can chase me down and strap me into it before I get away."

"That's outside the twelve-mile limit, you know. Are you coming back?"

I laughed. "If I have to swim."

"I'm serious. I need your statement. You aren't going to fly back to New York all of a sudden or something like that, are you?"

"Ross," I said, "I am leaving my beloved Cadillac Fleetwood geriatric sedan outside, and I would sooner abandon my own mother."

He smiled. "Okay. But give me a call as soon as you get back, okay?"

"I will."

"And don't let these Texas hooraws push you too far. There's a storm brewing. Around here, this time of year, they can be bad. Be on dry land before it gets here, you hear?"

"I hear."

The deputy returned and gave me the shoulder holster. I took off my jacket and strapped it on.

Outside, there came an eggbeater sound.

Grover Ellis got up. He adjusted his pistol belt. "Charlie'll land down on the beach. Let's go."

I followed him. Charity got up, too.

"Hold on," I said. "You're staying here."

Lisa Dantzler said, "I hired you both."

"There's work to be done here, too."

"I'm coming, Ben," Charity told me. "So stop arguing."

The MBI photographers were working outside. When they saw us coming, they threw the canvas over the torn remains of Millie Wiggins. None of us spoke. Except for the rising wind, it was very quiet.

"Aren't you forgetting something?" Charity asked.

How about that? After all my concern, I'd left the .38 upstairs.

"Harvey," Gautier said to one of his deputies, "let Mr. Shock borrow your gun."

The deputy handed me a heavy blue steel revolver. "Take care of it," he said. "That ain't state property."

"With my life," I promised. I tucked it in the shoulder holster. I felt like Sam Spade.

I have never been fond of helicopters. This one was big and looked sturdy. At least it had a floor, instead of that plastic bubble the smaller ones have wrapped around their front. I flew in small police choppers twice on assignments, and the shoot-outs that possibly awaited us at the end of the trip scared me less than the flight itself.

On the chopper's side a white name read, "Gulf Coast Flight Service," and there was a picture of a sea gull carrying a briefcase in his claws.

The pilot was standing near his aircraft. Grover introduced us. "This here's Charlie Blakemore," he said. "He

63

runs a ferry service out of Gulfport. Miz Charity Tucker, Ben Shock."

Charlie Blakemore nodded. "We better get started," he said. "The glass is dropping. I think old lady Hilda's getting ready to move. They're calling her a hurricane now."

"We could come back later," I said. Charity dug me in the small of the back, and I got aboard.

When we were strapped in, Blakemore lifted the chopper off the beach and skimmed over the breakers, gaining altitude.

Now I remembered another thing I don't like about helicopters. Instead of flying straight and level like any normal plane, they tend to *lean*. You are hanging from your straps and looking almost straight down at mother earth, and that is a scenic view I do not really admire.

"How far out is the tower?" I asked, mostly to keep my mind off my stomach, which was already protesting.

"Not far. Ten minutes or so. It's out eighteen miles. The shelf's gentle here. Bugs Bunny's in only two hundred feet of water."

"Who's in two hundred feet of water?" Charity asked.

"Bugs Bunny. The tower."

"I thought it was called Offshore Two."

Charlie Blakemore looked over his shoulder and smiled at her. I wished he would put his eyes back on the instrument panel where they belonged. He said, "Oh, that's what the Dantzler Company calls it. It's their number two rig. But the men put the name Bugs Bunny on it, because from a distance, the two rigging booms look like rabbit ears."

"Isn't that it up ahead?" I said.

He turned back to his flying. "No, it's too soon. I don't see anything."

Neither had I. But at least now he was facing front again.

"Is there much oil around here?" Charity asked.

Grover Ellis answered: "We think so. The test borings have been promising. This is the third time we've put down in this box, and we haven't hit the pool yet, but we've been getting closer."

"What do you mean, box?"

"It's the lease we have from the state. Three miles by three miles. We call it a box. Competing companies have other boxes. We can drill as many as six holes from one location, going out at an angle, before we have to abandon it and move."

I asked, "How do you move a rig like that around?"

"We float it. Bugs Bunny has been towed around the world. They built him in Liverpool, and the first place he worked was the North Sea, off Holland. Then they towed him around the Cape of Good Hope and set up operations in the Persian Gulf. After that, he worked off Galveston for a while, and now old Bugs is here."

"There he is, straight ahead," said Charlie Blakemore.

I peered out through the window. Yes, I saw it now. A dark shape against the horizon, a triangular metal arrow, perched on four tripod-like stilts of metal.

Charlie was right. The drilling platform looked like Bugs Bunny standing up to his neck in the Gulf of Mexico.

8

THE HELICOPTER banked and circled the Texas Tower. The landing pad was marked with a white circle painted on its deck. As we came closer, I saw a team of men working, stringing heavy ropes around the edge of the platform.

"Getting set for Hilda," said Blakemore, reducing the chopper's power. We sank toward the white circle. The wind gusted us slightly, and he corrected.

Now we were below the tops of the four heavy metal supports on which the platform rested.

"Those are the spuds," said Grover Ellis. "Once we reach our location, they're extended to the bottom and then we crank the tower up them, just like the ratchets on the bumper jack that comes with your car."

I shuddered. I would no more use a bumper jack on my Fleetwood than I would corrupt her innards with lead-free gasoline.

The helicopter bounced gently, and then the sound of rotors began to wind down.

"We're here," declared Charlie Blakemore. "And I

hope you don't plan to stay too long. Hilda might give us a couple of days yet, but she might also be here this afternoon."

Now that the chopper's engine was shut down, I could hear the heavy metallic sound of the tower's drills. It was a constant, shuddering noise that seemed to come through your feet as much as through your ears.

A huge derrick loomed over us, and hanging from its top was a giant block and tackle. From it danced a length of pipe.

"Are you going to drill right through the storm?" I asked.

Ellis shrugged. "If it gets too bad, we take the men off. But if we're still here, we work."

"I presume your BOP is installed," said Charity.

Ellis gawked. "How do you know about Blow-out Preventers?"

"I covered the Santa Barbara oil spill."

"I didn't," I said. "What the hell are you two talking about?"

"The BOP's a gadget that shuts off oil or gas that's trying to escape under pressure," said Grover Ellis. "They're standard on all offshore rigs these days."

"Except," Charity said sweetly, "that sometimes the teams forget to hook them up because of the time and money involved."

"Well, Dantzler Oil doesn't forget," Ellis grumbled. "Come on, I'll show you around."

68

As we circled the top deck of the platform, he said, "Our normal work crew is forty-eight men. There's three tours. Two work on board while the third one is on shore leave. Every week we switch, so the normal tour spends two weeks on Bugs, then a week ashore. Twelve-hour shifts, seven days a week."

"The overtime must be fantastic," I said.

He shrugged. "You can't run this kind of operation on shore rules. But there's plenty of dough for anyone who wants to work."

He nodded up at the drilling derrick. I saw men moving rapidly around a small platform. "We got a driller, three floormen and a derrickman up there, stringing the pipe. They'll drop seven hundred and twenty feet a shift. We work together like cogs in a machine. We have to. If one man slacks off a little, his shiftmates have to pull harder. And that won't do. We drill fourteen hundred and forty feet a day or I know the reason why."

"But you've been having trouble," Charity said. "What kind?"

"Little things. Any one of them could be carelessness. But as many as we've had—no, there's no way this crew could be *that* careless. Somebody's deliberately gumming up the operation."

We walked along the edge of the deck. Racks of pipe were piled over most of its surface. There were long rows of drilling bits. I wondered if Howard Hughes owned them all. Brightly painted toolboxes lined the passageway.

69

At one end, rows of deckhouses and trailers were lashed to the platform.

"Crew quarters, the day room and mess hall," said Ellis. "A man gets off duty, there's a meal waiting. We've got five cooks. And they're good. We serve more steak out here than they do at the biggest restaurant in Gulfport. Every six hours, a meal's there if the men want it."

Intrigued, Charity said, "What do they do for amusement? Is the fishing any good?"

"We wouldn't know," said Ellis. "When you've danced on an oil-slick floor inches away from a whirling rotary table for twelve hours, the only amusement you appreciate is sleep."

"I suppose there isn't any booze allowed out here," I said.

"You suppose right. Most accidents happen during the shift after the men get back from shore leave. You can't dull your reflexes and expect to survive on a drilling platform."

"You were talking about little accidents that you think might have been deliberate," prompted Charity.

"Yeah," he said. "Silly crap, like you'd expect from a crew of weevils."

"What's a weevil?" I asked.

"That's what we call green men. Come on over here."

We followed him to the edge of the platform. There was a guard rail, and strung along it now were sections of rope. The Gulf of Mexico was a good fifty feet below us. As I

70

have said, this is not my favorite way of looking at the ocean. I grabbed onto the guard rail.

"See that big tank down there full of brown stuff?"

I nodded. It looked like mud.

It was. Ellis said, "That's drilling mud."

"What do you use it for?"

"We pump it down the hole to contain pressure. We can hold back fifteen thousand pounds per square inch with mud. After that, we have to pour concrete. We don't like pouring concrete. It slows down our drill rate, and if we don't get our fourteen hundred and forty per day, we don't get our performance bonus."

"What happened?" asked Charity.

"The specific gravity of that mud has to be right on the money. If it's too light, it won't hold down the pressure and that could mean a blowout. If that happens and we don't get the BOPs shut in time, we could have an oil spill, at the best. At the worst, there could be an explosion and the whole tower might go up."

"And somebody altered the density of your mud balance?"

Ellis nodded. "We caught it in time. My mud foreman is a good man. He doesn't believe in machines. We've got an automatic mud balance, and it's hooked up to all kinds of gauges and alarm bells. But Steve still gives the mud the old manual examination every couple of hours. He caught a thin mixture just before we sent it down the hole."

"What else?" Charity prodded.

71

"Like I said, nothing you could point to. Tools left lying where they might fall down into one of the mud pumps, or into a generator. We're power-hungry out here. We've got six AC generators and three for DC. We could lose one of each and we'd get by. Two, and we'd be in trouble. So far, we've been lucky. Like I said, it's a good crew. They've caught most of this stuff before it could happen. The last bad one we had was day before yesterday. We had a twist-off and had to fish for the drill bit. We're down almost nine thousand feet, and drilling out at an angle. It took us more than an hour to get the fish out of the hole, and that was all down time. We're just catching up with the drill rate this morning. The most the men can speed up is five, maybe seven seconds a section, so it takes a long time to make up for an hour of down."

A klaxon horn sounded. Ellis looked up. The men on the drill tower were grouped around a section of pipe.

"Trouble," said Ellis. "Look, just wander around. The men know you're working for Miss Lisa. Ask whatever you want. I've got to get up there."

He scrambled up a steel ladder like a denim-clad monkey. It's always a little disconcerting to see a man on the job after you have formed a private opinion of him in a social situation. In Lisa Dantzler's dining room, Grover Ellis had seemed arrogant, hostile and more than a little shifty. Here, he was a tough professional, doing his job with skill and sound judgment.

The wind had died. The water was still a dull gray slick.

There were no whitecaps. What slight swell there was lapped gently against the steel spuds that held the platform off the ocean floor.

"I don't buy the ecology people sabotaging this rig," said Charity. "Demonstrating, court battles, letters to the editor, yes. But it takes a special knowledge to find your way around one of these drilling platforms. I wouldn't know where to start."

Remembering her question about the blow-out preventer, I said, "You seem to do all right."

"A warehouse of trivia, that's me." She looked around. "You just tell the filling station man to put in ten gallons of high test. You never think about people being out here, rooting it out of the earth."

"In this case, the water," I said. "And maybe we'd better do a little rooting of our own. I think our intrepid airman, Charlie Blakemore, is getting restless down there."

"Let's look up the mess hall and get some coffee," she said. "I know we're supposed to be the experts and all that, but looking around this platform, I don't know where to begin."

"You hit it," I said. "When in doubt, head for the coffee wagon."

I guess all mess halls are struck from the same mold, whether they're operated by the Army, the Navy, or the Dantzler Oil Company. Big tables laden with oversized containers of salt, pepper, sugar, milk and Heinz 57 Sauce.

There was a white-coated steward on duty, and he guessed what was on our minds the moment we entered, said, "Coffee?" and, at my nod, hurried to pour it into heavy, handleless mugs.

"Wow," I said, sipping the scalding coffee. "Don't put a spoon in yours. It'll melt. Charity, my love, we are being punished for our sins."

"Our biggest sin to present," she said sourly, "seems to be ineptitude. Ben, we're going to have to get this case in focus."

"That's what one of the two little southern girls said when the traveling photographer sat them down before his big old-fashioned view camera and ducked under the black cloth. 'What he goin' to do?' asked one. 'He gone focus,' said the other. 'Boaf us?' said the first."

"Barf," said my girl. "All right, Ben. Let's lay it out. Lisa owns a controlling interest in Dantzler Oil. Right?"

"Once Millie's will is probated, I would assume so. Excepting what husband Nick got, of course."

Charity shook her head. "There's a matter of trusts, too. Lisa told me about them last night. Sixty percent of the stock is locked up there, releasable only to the ultimate heirs after Lisa and Millie are gone."

"Well," I said through another mouthful of the vile brew, "Millie's gone already."

"Right. But how? Accidentally?"

"When was the last time you accidentally jumped into a swimming pool stark naked?"

"But why did she?"

74

"I told you. She was spaced out."

"And Lisa didn't even know. Millie was in the house? *How* did she get there? There weren't any extra cars lying around. And more important, Ben."

"What?"

"*Who* did Millie expect to meet out at the pool?"

9

I GUESS we talked to around a dozen guys in blue denim pants and surplus navy shirts. They were friendly, but not very helpful.

"This box is a jinx," one said. "We never had any trouble over Texas way."

"What else is different here?" I asked.

He looked at Charity. "Don't mind me," she said.

"Well," he said, embarrassed. "I don't think this has anything to do with the trouble we've been having. But most of the guys don't like the shore leave. Back in Texas, we had our own friends, you know?"

"Lady friends?" said Charity.

"Yes ma'am. Around here, there's so many shipyard workers and Air Force boys, the supply doesn't meet the demand, if you get what I mean. You don't find that many girls willing to wait around for two weeks out of three while her guy is out on Bugs Bunny. It makes things rough."

"Rough enough so that some of the boys might want to see this operation shut down?" I asked.

He stiffened. "No, sir! Nobody gripes longer or harder than an oilman. But not a one of us would ever drop a foot of drilling on purpose. That ain't our way. If we got so fed up we couldn't take the rig any more, we'd just blow. There's plenty of work for a good towerman."

"Well," Charity said, after he'd gone, "*somebody's* doing it."

"It might just be an unlikely series of accidents," I suggested.

"Just as Millie Wiggins was?" Charity shook her head. "Damn it, Ben, we've got to get hold of this one. Where's the motive? Who benefits if Bugs Bunny shuts down?"

"Why don't you get on the ship-to-shore and get some of your far-flung TV buddies working?" I said. "Maybe there's local gossip we ought to know."

"I'll get Charlie to let me use his radio," she said. "I don't think I want to go through the rig's communications room."

"Okay," I said. "Meanwhile, I'll keep checking around."

I hit pay dirt the third try. Maybe it was being alone that helped. There is undeniably something about Charity Tucker that turns even the toughest roustabout into a would-be gentleman, sneaking a shine on his work shoes by rubbing them up and down his trouser legs.

His name was Guy Pritchard. He was, he told me, assistant mud foreman. And at first he didn't have anything to say.

"Look," I said, "we're working with Ellis. He said you

77

all had instructions to cooperate."

"But I don't know anything," said Pritchard.

"Hasn't anything rubbed you the wrong way recently? Something you couldn't put a finger on, but it just seemed wrong?"

"Well," Pritchard said slowly.

"Go on."

"It didn't even happen out here."

"That doesn't matter."

"Well, I'm married. But it don't pay to bring my family all the way over here for a job that'll only last a year or so. Every six weeks, I go back to Galveston for my leave. But it's expensive, flying. So the shore leave in between, I spend here. I like fishing, and I drink a few beers, but I don't play around. You know what I mean?"

I knew what he meant, and nodded.

"Well, I take me a cabin at Bellavia's Fishing Camp."

"Where's that?"

"Just over the river, toward Pascagoula. Bellavia's got boats for rent, and bait, and his cabins are clean and cheap. I can get a boat and a motor and bait and a place to sleep cheaper than I'd pay a motel just for rent. But lately—"

He stopped. A bell was ringing up on the derrick. "I gotta go," he said. "They're getting ready to rev up the drill again."

"What time are you off duty?"

He looked at his watch. "Half an hour."

"I'll buy you a cup of coffee."

78

"Okay," he said, hurrying away.

The platform began to reverberate again under the sound of the heavy drill. I climbed down a hatch and went back to the mess hall. The second cup of coffee was no better than the first had been, but it was hot.

Charity joined me. "I found a friend of a friend," she said. "A sales rep for WWL in New Orleans. He's checking around, and I'll call him when we get ashore."

I told her what Pritchard had started to tell me about the fishing camp.

"He saw something," I said. "These guys out here aren't gossips. If it was something big enough to make Guy Pritchard uneasy, it's probably big enough to check out."

Grover Ellis came over. "Sorry," he said. "We found a section of pipe that had corroded out just enough to snap under pressure. It probably would have happened four or five thousand feet down, when the torque builds up, and then we'd have had to yank all that pipe to replace it."

"Another one of your accidents?" I said.

"Could be," he admitted. "Acid corrosion looks just like rust, after a day or two in this salt air."

"We may have found something," I said. "One of your men, Pritchard. He saw something down at a fishing camp—"

"Bellavia's?"

"That's the one."

He leaned forward. "What was it?"

"I don't know. He's going to meet me here when he

79

comes off shift and we'll find out."

Ellis nodded several times vigorously. "Good, good," he said. "Maybe I misjudged you, Shock. You know how to get things done." He nodded again. "Yes," he said. "That's good work."

"What's the word on Hilda?" I asked.

"Latest weather report puts her smack-dab over Cuba," he said. "The hurricane track has changed in the past few years. Used to be, we could count on them going up east of Florida and turning out to sea. Maybe they'd turn inland and bust up over the Carolinas. Nowadays, though, you can't be sure. They're just as likely to head right up the Gulf as not."

"Well," I said thoughtfully, "are you making plans to take the men off?"

"Don't have to make plans," he said shortly. "We've already got 'em. If things look bad, there's a trawler standing by off Ship Island."

The platform shuddered under the constant impact of the drill. I was glad I didn't have to endure its monotony two weeks at a time.

Then the monotony was broken. The klaxon sounded again. Three times.

Ellis leaped up. "Man in the water!" he shouted.

The mess hall emptied. We followed Ellis out onto the platform.

Two oilmen were hanging over the rail on the downwind side. A third was handing them life rings, which they threw.

"Who is it?" Ellis gasped, pounding up. I was right behind him.

"Pritchard," said one of the men.

I looked over. The assistant mud foreman was clutching one of the floating rings and fending his way off a metal spud with his feet. The swell had gotten higher in the past few minutes.

"Get me out!" he bawled at the top of his voice.

"Hang on!" yelled Ellis. "Get a rope over here. Move!"

One of the oilmen rushed over with a coil of hemp rope. He secured one end to the railing and heaved the other down into the water.

"Kick your way free!" shouted Ellis. "Tie that rope around your waist."

Pritchard struggled toward the safety of the rope.

One of the men yelled a warning.

A shark's fin had cut the surface of the water near the swimming man.

"Shark!" called another worker.

Pritchard swam harder.

"Don't kick up that water!" bellowed Ellis. "Take it easy."

I shoved Charity back. "Don't watch," I said.

"What about you?" she shot back. "Are you wearing that pistol for decoration?"

I hauled out the deputy's gun.

"Be careful!" someone warned. "Don't hit Pritchard."

The shark was gone now. For a moment it looked as if Guy Pritchard would reach the rope and rescue.

81

Then the dorsal fin reappeared. It was very close to the swimming man. There wasn't enough to shoot at, but I squeezed off a round. The bullet sent a spout of water up just behind the creature.

"Give me that thing!" ordered Grover Ellis. He snatched the pistol.

Pritchard saw the shark and shrieked. It wasn't circling as sharks usually do. Instead, it closed steadily on the terrified man.

Ellis fired. I couldn't tell where the bullet went.

The shark didn't hit Pritchard the way the one in the pool had hit Millie Wiggins. Instead, it seemed to grasp him and then lay motionless in the water, dragging his head under.

Every time he broke the surface, Pritchard screamed. Ellis fired again. Two more sharks appeared. They streaked in toward the helpless man. They were hungrier than their buddy. They rolled, showing white belly, and tore great chunks of bloody flesh out of the screaming man.

The water was roiled with foam and crimson.

Pritchard's voice was one constant shriek now. Between the piercing cries of pain, he pleaded, "God! Shoot me! Please, somebody shoot me!"

Ellis rested both hands on the railing, held his breath, and shot him.

10

CHARITY and I sat in the communications shack with Ellis. He had just finished radioing the report of Pritchard's death to shore. Somewhere, the radioman found a bottle of Old Crow. Ellis didn't comment on it, just gulped down a heavy slug.

"I was trying to shoot the shark," he repeated for the third time.

"Don't torment yourself," said Charity. "That poor man was dead. Nothing could have saved him."

"Do you have many sharks around here?" I asked.

"You see a few," he said, still working on the booze. "The smaller fish eat the garbage, and then the sharks show up and eat them."

The radioman leaned forward and lifted the bottle out of his numbed fingers. "Save some for daddy," he said, and drank.

"Stan," mumbled Ellis, "what's the latest weather?"

"Hilda's breaking loose from Cuba," said the radioman. "Small craft warnings are going up from Galveston to Key West."

"Then they figure she's coming inside?"

"That's the way it looks."

"Okay," said Ellis, standing up and shaking his head. He seemed to be shaking off the events of the past few moments. His voice became crisper. "Contact the trawler. Get her out here. Alert the men. We're going to Storm Alert. I've got to go ashore. I'll keep in touch. If I give you a shutdown, I want everybody on board that trawler in five minutes."

"What if we lose contact?" asked the radioman.

"I'll leave word with the shift foremen," said Ellis. "If the wind gets up above fifty knot gusts, it's an automatic shutdown and get the hell to shore."

"I think that's smart," agreed the radioman.

"Let's go," said Ellis, leading the way toward the helicopter.

Blakemore was glad to see us.

"Hilda's broken free of Cuba," he said.

"We heard," Ellis answered. "Let's get back to Singing River."

Did I tell you how little fun it is riding a helicopter? That applied to calm, smooth skies. Try it sometime when the gusts of wind are enough to shudder the airship and make its rotors groan as they claw at the turbulent air. My seat belt bit deep into my belly and Charity's hand gripped my wrist so hard I was afraid I'd lose circulation in my hand.

"Better give me back the pistol, Grover," I said. "It belongs to one of Gautier's deputies. He's going to be very happy to hear what happened to it."

Ellis gave it to me. "It shoots high," he said sourly.

"Why didn't you use your own?" I asked

He looked down at the Ruger strapped to his leg. He laughed and slipped it from the holster. He spun the cylinder, put the barrel to his head and squeezed the trigger.

Charity screamed.

The hammer fell.

There was only a dull click.

"It's empty," he said. "I never keep it loaded."

"Then why carry it?"

He spread his hands. "Habit. It's part of the costume."

I didn't believe him, but I said, "Men have been killed for carrying an empty gun that scared somebody else."

"Hell," he said. "It started out in the Persian Gulf. Everybody there went around armed. I did, too. Then when we set up off Texas, the guys started riding me because I was naked. So I put the gun on again. Only it's a single-action, and I was afraid of shooting myself in the leg. That's why I carry it unloaded. I figured if I ever wanted to shoot a sea gull or something, there would be time to load it up."

"But there wasn't today," I said.

"No," he said, looking down at the empty gun in his hand. "There sure wasn't."

I asked Blakemore, "Can you set this thing down in Singing River before you go out to The Old Place?"

"Sure," he said. "There's a pad out behind the police station."

85

"Well, that's where we want to go," I said.

"Why?" asked Ellis.

"Don't you think somebody ought to return the deputy's pistol before he comes looking for it? Besides, Gautier wants a statement from me about last night."

"Oh," he said.

The rest of the trip was silent, except for the shuddering rivets in the helicopter and the even louder knocking of my knees.

We made the landing behind Singing River's police station without any problems. Grover Ellis stayed in the chopper to fly on over to report to Lisa Dantzler. Charity and I went inside.

The first man I saw was the deputy whose gun I'd borrowed.

I handed it back to him along with the shoulder holster. "You'd better reload," I said.

"Huh?"

"And it shoots high." I looked around. "Where's the Chief?"

"Up on Beach Street," said the deputy. "You might find him in the Sea Gull. He has lunch there."

"Okay," I said. "Thanks."

"Why didn't you tell him about Pritchard?" Charity asked when we were back on the street.

"What's the point? He'd only want us to talk to Gautier anyway."

The late morning air was heavy and oppressive. I decided that if I ever came to Mississippi again, it would not be in August. Particularly an August when a hurricane was lurking around somewhere out there in the Gulf of Mexico.

"Ben," said Charity. "Do sharks often do that?"

"You mean attack?"

"No. That first one—he seemed to be holding Pritchard so the other sharks could feed."

"I've never heard of it before," I said. "But I'm not exactly the shark expert. They feed in packs. I know that. But they aren't supposed to be the brightest creatures in the sea. Porpoises beat the hell out of them all the time, using their brains instead of their teeth."

"Why sharks all of a sudden? First in Lisa's swimming pool, and then out at the tower. A savage school of sharks."

"Sharks don't go to school," I said halfheartedly.

"If you're not going to work on this case," Charity said grimly, "you might as well drive back to New York."

I stopped in the middle of the sidewalk. "Listen, baby," I said, "don't show your fangs at me. I'm working just as hard in my way as you are in yours. And I'm just as frustrated, so don't come on like Chief Ironsides with me."

She slipped her arm in mine. "Thanks," she said dryly. "I needed that." We walked half a block. "Ben, seriously, I've never felt so much at sea."

"You need a rest," I said. "We both need a rest. We need some of Uncle Jeff's catfish and hushpuppies and home-brew."

She laughed and said, "Uncle Jeff's up in Kentucky. But they serve catfish here. I saw a sign on the highway as we drove in last night."

"It won't be the same. How could anyone outcook Uncle Jeff?"

The town wasn't crowded for a Saturday morning. The stores were small, and neat, and empty. We passed two bars. At least, I supposed they were bars. The windows were painted over, but there were Jax and Old Milwaukee signs hanging above the doors. As we passed the third one, the door slammed open and a man came catapulting out. He landed at my feet, flat on his back. He was a runny-eyed, red-nosed, very drunk man of perhaps sixty. His clothes were old and faded. He did not look to be the Mayor of Singing River.

I bent over. "Let me help you up, old-timer," I said.

Another voice said, "Back off there, mister."

I turned. A younger man, wearing overalls and a straw hat, stood in the door. He was holding a tiny .22 pistol. It was one of those made-in-Italy $9.95 Saturday Night Specials. The kind the politicians hold up to the TV camera when they call for gun control, and the kind that every law-abiding hunter and sportsman wishes were never allowed to be sold, because the newspapers and the anti-gun lobbies lump his expensive sporting weapon in along with them. There's only one reason a man carries a Saturday Night Special—to shoot somebody, either in self-defense, or anger, or malice. The first reason is usually the least used.

"Don't point that popgun at me, friend," I said.

"I ain't pointing it at anybody," he said, swinging open the cylinder and dumping the shells out onto the sidewalk. They were .22 shorts, solid points. If they were to hit you in the leg, they'd go right through with hardly more of a hole than a knitting needle might make. If they hit you in the head or the heart, you would die as quickly as if a howitzer was aimed at you. Bobby Kennedy was killed with a .22 short.

The younger man bent over and placed the empty pistol on the ground near the older man and said, "You ever pull that thing on me again, Krebs, and I'll shove it down your throat."

He turned and went back inside the bar.

I looked at Charity. She made an elaborate shrug.

Chief Ross Gautier arrived. He scowled down at the man on the sidewalk.

"Howdy, Chief," said the man called Krebs.

"Get the hell up," said Gautier.

Krebs got up.

"Pick up your pistol."

Krebs picked it up.

"Now, empty it out."

"It's already empty," Krebs said. "Old Sparky, he stripped her clean."

Gautier took the gun, checked the cylinder and the chamber and nodded. He handed it back to Krebs.

"Okay," he said. "Go ahead."

"Ross, please," said Krebs. "I'm tapped out. I paid me

ten dollars for this pistol."

"Do it," said Gautier.

Krebs scowled. He lifted his arm and, with all his might, threw the pistol against the sidewalk. Being a cheap cast-iron Italian-made typical Saturday Night Special, it did precisely what it might have done in his hand had he ever fired it.

It broke into little pieces.

"Now," said Gautier, "you go on down to the jailhouse and turn yourself in to the desk man for littering and pay the fine. You got the two dollars?"

"I ain't got two bits," said Krebs. "Now I can't buy me another pistol until payday—"

Gautier dug into his pocket and took out two crumpled one-dollar bills. He gave them to the old man.

"You do like I said, you hear? I'll have Higgenbotham hold this back from your pay. And I'll tell you something else, you better not go buying no more of these cheap guns. It's an expensive habit."

Krebs scowled and weaved up the street toward the police station, holding the dollar bills in one hand like a tiny green flag.

"Come on inside," said Gautier. "I'll buy you-all a beer. I got to talk to Sparky."

We went in. It was dark and cool and there was the rich aroma of malt and hops. A real beer joint.

The bar ran the length of the room. Leaning up against it were several men, including the young one in overalls who had thrown Krebs out the front door. A garish juke box was blaring out "Welfare Cadillac" with bone-shaking volume. Two young oilmen were playing shuffleboard on one of those machines that lets you knock down bowling pins.

As we entered, the young overalled man looked up.

"Howdy, Sherf," he said

"Morning, Sparky," said Ross Gautier. "Buy you a beer?"

"My treat," said Sparky. "These friends of yours?"

"You might say that," Gautier answered.

Sparky gave me a slight wave of the hand. "Sorry I mouthed off at you," he said. "But I didn't want nobody getting between me and old man Krebs. He's a mean little bastard. I got his pistol, but he might of been carrying a knife, too."

"You didn't rough him up any, did you?" asked Gautier.

"Hell no. Listen, Sherf, I was just sitting here, minding my own business and talking to Lucy." He nodded toward the heavy-set barmaid, who had set down four bottles of Old Milwaukee beer. Sparky passed them out, said to Lucy, "Glass for the lady."

Lucy dipped under the bar and came up with a glass which looked as if it had been sitting around there since the Civil War. Pointedly, Charity drank from the bottle.

"Anyways," Sparky went on, "old Krebs come in spoiling for trouble. It ain't no secret that I'm worried the oil operation out there might mess up my shrimping, and I reckon I spoke out against it pretty strong. But there

91

weren't no call for him to come down on me like a ton of bricks and call me everything but a yellow dog, just cause I said that even if oil *was* bringing money into Singing River, *I* wasn't getting any of it."

"Two sides to every question," said Gautier. "What then?"

"Well, I started to walk around him. I do that once for any man, Sherf. Ask anybody. They'll tell you ole Sparky'll walk around trouble every time, if you give him the chance."

"But he wouldn't let you?"

"He stuck himself right out there in front of me. I told him, 'Krebs, I stepped around you once. I ain't going to do it again.' And that's when he pulled out his pistol."

Gautier frowned. "Did he have it concealed?"

Sparky hesitated. It was obvious to all of us that he was getting ready to say "yes." But then he shook his head. "No, sir, Sherf, I don't think so. He had it out in the open. I just didn't notice."

He drank deeply and finished the bottle of beer. "You want to run me in for rousting him?"

"No," said Gautier. "But walk around him a second time if you run up against him, you hear?"

"I'll sure do that," said Sparky. "I don't want no trouble, you know that, Sherf."

"Well," said Gautier, "you be good. If you can't be good, be careful."

Sparky laughed. "Yes, sir, Sherf, I'll do that little thing." He bobbed his head at us. "Pleased to make your acquaintance. Well, I got to get to work. Got me a couple of cases of shrimp to head."

He bobbed his head again and left.

"Seems like a nice enough fellow," I said.

Gautier put his bottle of beer down on the bar with a heavy thump. "That nice fellow," he said, "killed two Bay St. Louis men five years ago for poaching on his crayfish traps. I know it, and the whole town knows it, but we ain't got no proof."

"My, my, my," I said, echoing the familiar refrain of an old friend, Chief Miles Cook of Pilgrim's Pride, Mass.

"Do you think he might be mad enough at the oil people to take some kind of action against them?" asked Charity.

Gautier shook his head. "Not Sparky. He's got a temper hot as a branding iron. But he'd never sit down and plan out trouble against somebody."

"Too bad," she said, sipping her beer from the neck of the bottle. "Because we're fresh out of suspects."

"What happened out there in the Gulf?" asked the Chief. "I heard there was an accident on the tower."

"Another run-in with sharks," I said. I described Guy Pritchard's death.

Gautier swore. "With my deputy's gun? That ain't going to make the coroner happy."

"Ellis said he was trying to hit the shark," I said. "It may be the truth. But I'll tell you, Chief, if I'd been holding the pistol, I might have tried to put that poor bastard out of his misery, too. There wasn't any hope for him."

"I hear what you're saying," said Gautier. "It just messes up the case, that's all. Nothing we can't handle."

Charity leaned over the bar and studied the display of assorted merchandise behind it. It seemed that in a Singing River beer joint, you could buy: razor blades, combs, fingernail clippers, pocket flashlights, Timex watches, fishing lures, toothpaste, shaving cream, hair tonic, pocket knives, lighter fluid, flints, the lighters themselves, handkerchiefs, little Mississippi license plates with various names on them, and—in assorted sizes—men's jockey shorts.

"Is that a punchboard?" Charity asked.

"Sure is, honey," said Lucy. "Brand-new one, only one prize took off it."

Delighted, my girl said, "I'm a sucker for punchboards. How much?"

"Three holes for a quarter."

"Give me six," Charity said, holding out her hand. I put a Kennedy half dollar in it. That was something else we'd noticed about the south. Instead of hoarding half dollars, the people down here spent them.

"Three more beers, too," said Gautier. I reached for my pocket and he shook his head. "No, no. These are on me."

As Lucy rummaged for the beers, Charity took up the big heart-shaped punchboard and, chuckling with delight, shoved the key through six holes in various locations.

"How many punches do you figure that board has?" I asked Gautier.

"Four, five hundred."

"And prizes?"

"Ten."

"Not very good odds."

"Not very," he agreed.

Charity was unrolling the little twists of paper and comparing them with the winning numbers printed at the top of the card. "Shhh," she said.

"I thought punchboards were illegal," I said.

"Could be," said Gautier. "Since they don't hurt nobody, we don't worry about them. Of course," he added, raising his voice toward Lucy, "if we found out the bar owner had a secret index and was punching out the winners for himself, we might not look too kindly on it."

"You know better than that, Ross Gautier," she said, thumping the beers down before us. "Sure, some of those boards have indexes. But we don't buy that kind. We do all right playing them honest."

"I won!" shrieked Charity, holding up a printed number. "Two hundred nine! It's a winner!"

Lucy examined the slip of paper and the winners at the top of the board. "You sure did," she said. "That's good for a three-pound fruit cake."

She plunked it on the bar. I opened the gaily decorated can and pressed my finger against the plastic-wrapped cake. It was as hard as a cement sidewalk.

"This thing is older than you are," I told Charity.

"Hush up," she said. "You have no gambling spirit."

We worked on our beers. In the back of my mind, and in Charity's, too, I was sure, was the realization that we

95

were deliberately ignoring our problems for a few moments, but that we would have to get back to them soon.

"Singing River's a beautiful name," said Charity to Gautier. "How did it come about?"

"It's an old legend," he said. "Originally, this part of the country was settled by the Pascagoula Indians. They were a branch of the Chocktaw nation. Good people, I understand. So good that when they became friendly with the French, who originally settled here, then left for Louisiana in seventeen sixty-four, the Pascagoulas packed up and followed them. All they left behind was their name and the legend of the singing river."

"Lovely," said Charity. "I adore legends."

"It has to be a variation of Romeo and Juliet," I said. "All legends are."

Gautier grinned and nodded. "Romeo was really Altama, the son of the Pascagoula chief. And Juliet was Anola, a beautiful maiden who was promised to Otanga, chief of the Biloxi tribe. But Altama met up with her one day in the woods and fell in love. He kidnaped her, without much resistance, I'd imagine, and she made a big impression on the Pascagoula tribe. A big wedding ceremony was set up, but the night before the bash, the Biloxis swooped down on them. Altama offered to give himself up to the Biloxis, but the Pascagoula warriors wouldn't hear of it. When they saw that the Biloxis were bound to win, the whole tribe decided to walk into the river instead of surrendering."

96

"How beautiful," said Charity.

"The Japs did the same thing on Saipan," I said. "Nobody thought it was beautiful there."

"Shush," said my girl.

"Well," said Chief Gautier, lubricating his vocal cords with a generous swallow of Old Milwaukee, "first the old folks and the children marched into the river, singing their death chant. The warriors followed. Only Altama and Anola were left. They hugged each other one last time and, still singing, walked out and drowned. The story goes that ever since that night, the river sings their song when the wind is right and the spirit is willing."

"It's sheer poetry," said Charity.

"Also salami," I said. "How can a river sing?"

Gautier shrugged. "I don't know. But it does. I heard it myself once. It sounds just like a swarm of humming bees."

"Maybe that's just what it is," I suggested.

"Ben!" said Charity. "You have no heart!"

"That may be," I said. "I wonder what the Pascagoulas would do now if they saw their fishing grounds threatened by offshore oil developments?"

"Yeah," said Gautier. "Legends are nice. But the reality we've got today is what's split this coast into two factions. One side is all for the oil people. Hell, they've put lots of money into the economy down here—money we needed real bad. And if they hit it out there, we can have another boom again, one bigger than the Ingalls shipyard back in

97

the Second World War. But you've got a lot of tourist-type people living down here now, too. Some of them work for the Space program. Others are retired. They don't care how much the economy might be helped by an oil discovery. They've got theirs, and they don't really want this part of the country to get too prosperous, because then the prices would go up and they wouldn't be such big fish in a little pond."

"I somehow sense which side you're on," Charity said.

"Sure," said Gautier. "I don't take kindly to outsiders lording it over me just because they got money and I don't. That includes Miss Lisa, in case you didn't notice. I was born here and I grew up here. I aim to die here. This is my country. A cop, you look at his uniform, and that's all you see. You look at this khaki and my badge and my gun, and it wouldn't occur to you that I got a wife and three kids out in Moss Point. But I do. I want good schools for those kids, not the leftovers after they get through spending all the Federal money bussing for racial integration and blowing the budget on fancy new buildings instead of trained teachers and good books. Dantzler Oil may bring that kind of money in here; they pay taxes, they provide employment. My kids swam on the public beaches maybe five times last year. If there's a little oil spill, they can walk around it. If the price of shrimp goes up a dime a pound, it don't matter, because we don't boil shrimp that often anyway. So my view is, the hell with the tourists and the retired folks who want everything left the way it is. They don't have to grow with this town. Me and my kids, we do. End of speech and for Christ's sake, Lucy, give us three more."

"What do you think, honestly, Ross?" I said. "Was Millie Wiggins murdered? Did you get any answers out of Lisa or Nick?"

"Nary a one," he said, lapsing into a thick southern accent. "We cracker sherfs don't have the interrogation procedures down tight enough to trap those sharp city folks."

"Shove it," I said. "I'm not zinging you. I'm looking for help. Charity and me, we don't have a clue."

He straightened up. "Neither do I, Ben. According to the Dantzler household, nobody had the slightest idea Millie was there. She was supposed to be on one of her shopping sprees in Biloxi."

"Without her husband?"

"That was her usual mode of travel. Nick and Millie never were much for going around holding hands. He's been their lawyer for—"

"He's been *what?*" yelped Charity.

Puzzled, Gautier said, "Huh?"

"What did you say Nick's been?"

"The Dantzlers' lawyer. Hell, that's how he met Millie to begin with."

Charity looked at me. "He said he was in oil, didn't he?"

Thinking, I said, "Well, he was pretty drunk, baby. He said he was *sort* of in oil. Maybe he was being sarcastic.

It could have meant anything."

"The lawyer who called me said his name was Conrad."

"That fits," said Ross Gautier. "His full name is Nicholas Conrad Wiggins. But, shoot, Miss Charity, Nick's been a lawyer ever since I knew him. He went to Ole Miss, then he went up to Dartmouth, and finished at N.Y.U. in New York City. He set up business here in town for a while, but all that come his way was real estate closings, so he moved over to New Orleans. That's where he picked up the Dantzler business, and about a year later, he married Miss Millie."

"I will be a red-necked son of a bitch," I said. "That bastard suckered me in."

"Maybe so, maybe not," said Ross Gautier. "Old Nick, he ain't breathed a sober breath since he come back here with that offshore rig. Things ain't been right between him and his wife for quite some time. So like you said, he may have just been putting on the poor mouth when he told you he was an oilman. Hell, Nick *hates* oilmen. Some of us figure he hates oil*women,* too. But that's not news around here."

"It's news to me," I said. I looked at Charity. "Any ideas?"

"I don't know how important it is that Nick concealed his identity from me on that first call," she said slowly. "He didn't know we'd accept the job. He might have wanted to preserve as much anonymity as possible in case we didn't go along with the deal. And as the Chief has

100

pointed out, he was hardly in any condition last night to think clearly. It's a little odd piece of the puzzle, I'll admit. But I don't see where it fits. Not yet."

Gautier looked at his watch. "Whoops," he said. "Lunch is over."

"Sorry," I said. "I guess we kept you from having it."

He grinned. "No you didn't. I just drank it."

11

CHARITY and I each gave Gautier a statement, speaking into a cassette recorder on his desk.

When we were done, he said, "Thanks. I'll get this transcribed, and the next time you come by, you can sign it." He took out the little cassette and held it up to the light. "What the hell did we do before these things came along? It's getting so if you shut your eyes, the technology passes you by before you get them open again."

"What about those sharks?" I said. "Did you ever hear of that kind of behavior?"

"Not personally," he said. But you might drive out to Point Biloxi. It's only five, six miles. They got the Cape Distress Shark Research Laboratory there. Ask for Dr. Jerry Marconi."

"Shark research? What the hell for?"

"Don't ask me. Maybe there was a little government money laying around they didn't know what to do with. Hell, a friend of mine got a grant to grow marijuana for research. He put in nineteen acres up near Jackson."

"Sounds great. What happened to it?"

He laughed. "One night the guard fell asleep. On purpose or not, nobody knows. Anyway, somebody pulled up with a great big truck and a harvesting combine. They cut that weed and baled it up just like hay, and by dawn, they were long gone. We figure around two million bucks street value, and that's conservative. My friend is no longer in charge of agrarian research at Ole Miss. He's lucky not to be in the poky."

Sourly, Charity said, "Maybe we can get a government grant to send Ben and me through investigative training. It looks like we need all the help we can get."

"I think I'll shoot out to that shark joint," I said. "Why don't you call your buddy from WWL? I'll see you later." I turned to Ross Gautier. "Is there a taxi stand in town?"

"Over by the drugstore," Gautier said. "I'd lend you one of our cars, but they're all out right now. We're checking the empty houses to be sure they're secured for the storm."

"A cab's all right." I pecked Charity on the nose. "Perk up, lady. It's always darkest before the dawn."

Wearily, she said, "I'll see you back at The Old Place."

"In an hour or so," I agreed. I waved at Gautier, went across the street and tapped at the window of the tiny Black and White Taxi Co., Inc.

A skinny young man popped out. "Yes sir? Cab?"

"If you've got one."

"Oh, we do. Yes sir, indeed we do. Long haul or short?"

"I don't know. I'm going out to Point Biloxi."

He considered. "Well, I reckon that's what we'd call a

medium haul. Yes sir, medium."

"Are you the driver?"

"Sometimes. Mostly I'm the dispatcher. But today I'm the driver, too, yes sir, count of we're short-handed. Everybody's boarding up for the storm. Got to get ready."

"How come you aren't?"

He laughed. "Don't live here. My folks are over to Pascagoula, yes sir. I just work here. You wouldn't catch a Copeland living this side of the Singing River, no sir."

I sighed. "Is that your name? Copeland?"

"Yes sir. James Copeland, at your service. Just let me lock up this here office, and we'll be on our way."

He slipped a padlock through the hasp, clicked it shut, and gestured toward an ancient Nash parked nearby.

"Is *that* the Black and White Taxi Company's wonderful machine?" I asked.

"That's our Number Two cab," he said, smiling at it as if it were a Porsche. "Number One's over in New Orleans on a long haul. Oil feller, goes first class. Doesn't like to fly. Hires Number One ever time he has to make a business trip."

"Doesn't he ever hire Number Two?" I asked, surveying the decrepit Nash.

"Never once. Good thing. Yes sir, I'd be surprised if she'd make the trip. Third gear's mighty shaky. Keeps slipping out."

"What happens if you get a call while we're over at Point Biloxi?"

"I don't know. I never got any calls when I wasn't here.

So I never had to face the problem."

I decided to sit in the front seat with him. That way I could grab the wheel if he finished slipping over the edge. I crawled in beside him.

"Point Biloxi, we are *on* our way!" he yelled, turning the key.

Nothing happened.

"Oh," he said. He got out, unlocked the office door, went inside, and in a moment, reappeared carrying a battery. He popped the hood, installed the battery, and got back inside. This time the starter worked. Not very well, but it urged the engine to turn over slowly, and pretty soon it caught, and Copeland goosed the gas pedal until the engine was purring fairly smoothly.

"Forgot I had the battery inside there so's I could play the car radio," he explained.

I looked at the dash. There was a hole where the radio had once been.

"I see," I said. "You've got the car radio inside the office."

"I had me a portable Sony," he said. "But my sister took it back. Besides, you don't want to listen to the radio anyway, do you? If you do, I can put it back."

"No, no," I said. "Let's just be on our way."

He headed west on Route 90. Just as we left the town behind, the engine roared briefly. He hit the gear shift. "Slipped out," he said. "Sometimes I have to go all the way in second."

But he managed to get Number Two back into third. I

agreed with the nameless oil man. I wouldn't have wanted to try to make New Orleans in the Nash.

"You don't plan to stay long, do you?" Copeland said nervously. "What I mean, when we get a big storm like this Hilda that's coming, that point can go under water. Hard on a car's body. We have to fight rust, you know. Biggest problem in this salt air. Naval jelly works good, if you catch her before she rusts all the way through."

"An hour or so," I said.

"Have to put Number Two on waiting time, in that case. Two dollars an hour."

"Go ahead," I said.

"Is that too much?" he said anxiously. "We could go down to a dollar seventy-five if—"

"Two bucks is fine," I said. "Won't this thing go any faster?"

"Only if I hold her in third gear."

"I'll hold it," I said, taking hold of the shift lever. "See if we can get over forty."

We did. Forty-six, on a straight section of road.

"There's the turn, up ahead," said James Copeland. "You want to shift her down to second?"

I let go. "You can do it," I said.

"Thanks," he said, grinding off a few cogs as he tried, unsuccessfully, to double-clutch.

Just as we made the turn, the sun came out and it was as if we were driving down a yellow brick road as the seashells and sand sparkled against the dusty windshield.

"Maybe Hilda's not coming after all," I said.

106

Copeland shook his head. "No sir," he said. "This here is what they call the calm before the storm."

Almost as good as "It's always darkest before the dawn. . . ."

The Cape Distress Shark Research Laboratory was housed in a curious, castlelike building that looked as if it might be more at home overlooking the Mediterranean. The Nash pulled up and parked near the front door.

I got out. "You'll wait?"

"Unless it looks like we're going under water," said Copeland. "You can't expect me to risk having the car's body rust out. Bodywork costs money these days. Even naval jelly ain't as good as it used to be. No sir, you can't be too careful with this salt air."

"I'll hurry," I promised. "If things look too salty, come and get me."

"I'll do that thing," he said. Then he added, "If I have time, that is."

"Take time," I urged.

There wasn't any doorbell. But the door was unlocked. I went in. There was a receptionist's desk, but nobody was at it. The lights were on, however. And quiet FM music played in the background. It was the syrupy nothing music you always hear in office buildings and elevators.

A light box was mounted on one wall. Clipped to it were 8 × 10 transparencies. I looked at them closely. They were color photographs of sharks, taken from closer range than I would have enjoyed.

At one end of the room, a door beckoned. I accepted.

If they hadn't wanted me to enter, they wouldn't have left it unlocked. Right?

Of course, that's what Willie Sutton said, too.

I found myself in a darkened chamber, one whole wall of which was thick glass that looked into an illuminated tank of water.

It was full of sleek, gliding, dangerous-looking sharks.

I stepped closer to the glass wall.

So this was what they really looked like—tautly muscled death hovering motionlessly in the blueness of the water.

Then a new shape entered the pool.

It was a well-formed girl, dressed in a one-piece red bathing suit and wearing an air tank and mask. She swam down among the sharks as if they were old friends.

She had one of those underwater Nikor cameras. She poked it into the snouts of the sharks with a casual disregard of their teeth and deadly tails that raised the hackles on my neck.

She wasn't wearing a cap. Her hair floated freely. Although the water gave it a greenish hue, she was obviously a gorgeous blonde. I felt perversely glad that Charity wasn't here. My girl reacts unfavorably to other gorgeous blondes.

The blonde in the pool swam toward the glass in pursuit of a bashful shark, and there spotted me. Her eyes widened inside the mask. She made a gesture with her hand, a "wait there" motion, and vanished toward the surface.

The sharks eyed her departure much as a diner would

view the exit of his salad course.

A moment later, she appeared in the large room, tying the belt around a moisture-stained robe.

"Hello," she said. "I didn't know anybody was out here."

"The joint was empty," I said, "so I just walked in."

"I know," she said. "Everybody's upset about the hurricane. They're all at home taping up their windows."

"But you live in Moss Point and—" I began. She stared at me blankly. "Sorry," I said. "Bad joke."

I nodded toward the plate glass. "I noticed you were wearing a double-hose regulator. How come? These days, almost everybody goes for single-hose."

"Bubbles," she said.

"Who?"

"Air bubbles in the water. Single hoses have a second stage that lets the bubbles out where they might block your vision. In a tank of sharks, a second of obscured vision could mean good-by Dr. Marconi."

"Where is he?" I asked. "I came out here to—"

"I'm Marconi," she said.

"Jerry Marconi? I thought—"

"It's Jerri for Geraldine, ugh, which my proud parents inflicted on me at an early age and which I have tried to live down ever since. So how do you do, sir, and who may I ask are you?"

"Ben Shock," I said. "I'm helping the Dantzler Oil people out with a couple of accidental deaths which seem to involve sharks."

"Nick sent you," she said.

"No," I answered, puzzled. "Chief Gautier did. Do you know Nick Wiggins?"

"Off and on," she said, smiling. "But I know the Chief too. He's okay. What's the problem?"

I looked around the darkened room uneasily. "You're wet," I said. "Why don't you dry off, and maybe we can sit down and have a cup of coffee or something—"

"Something," she said. "My work's done. I can have a nip or two. I can use it. That tank's less than sixty degrees. I'd wear a wetsuit, but the sharks seem to be used to my golden tan and I'd hate to give them a look at something new that might seem good to eat."

"Lead the way," I said.

She did. We went into a small apartment behind the tank, where she poured each of us a short snifter of brandy and then retired behind a folding screen to change.

"Just like the movies," she said. "Except if you poke your nose over the screen and start sneering like George Sanders, I will poke you in the eye."

"I like what I already saw," I said honestly. "I don't want to risk losing an eye. I'll wait."

"Nice man," she said. "Where have you been all my life?"

"Walking a beat in New York City," I said.

"Cop?"

"Most of the past six years. Now I bounce around the country trying to bail out unpleasant people like Lisa Dantzler."

110

"Encore," she said, coming out in a short sun suit that left little to the imagination. In the slang of the Pascagoula Indians, she was built like a brick wickiup. "Miss Dantzler is not my favorite person either."

"But she's in trouble," I said. "Gautier thought you could give me some information about sharks."

"Ask," she said, pouring us each a generous snort of the fifty-year-old Martell.

I described Millie Wiggins' death.

Jerri Marconi frowned. "That's unusual," she said. "You don't often find sharks going into closed areas like that conduit. My pool here is sea-fed, but I have a wide channel entering it, closed off by metal nets. Even then, sometimes I have to use scent to get them back inside."

"Millie was the first one," I said. "Maybe just a horrible accident, maybe rigged some way. But this morning I saw another." I told her how Guy Pritchard had been held by the first shark while the others attacked.

"Sometimes the pack seems to work together," she mused. "I don't know if it's deliberate, but I've heard of the first shark immobilizing the victim while the pack-mates fed. Yet, there's a deliberate pattern of violence here. Sharks aren't all that brave. They're the garbage men of the sea. Dead meat's their dish. Nature knows better than man. Every creature has his place in the food chain. I don't admire sharks, but I respect them. And this behavior isn't in their pattern. Ben, I think you've got a clever murderer using sharks to do his dirty work."

"How?"

"I'm not sure. What kind of sharks were they?"

I shrugged. "Big and with lots of teeth. You know—you've seen one shark, you've—"

"—seen them all." She smiled. "Well, all sharks are dangerous, with the possible exception of the basking and whale sharks, which lack the cutting teeth the others have. But even among the others, there's a great variation. The most commonly known requiem shark—that's what we call a man-eater, the white shark—is usually found in the open ocean throughout the world. *Carcharodon carcharias*—"

"I gather that's his Sunday name."

"Just showing off," she said. "We'll call him Whitey."

"Very appropriate these days," I mumbled through my brandy. She noticed it was getting low, and replenished my snifter.

"Well, in one part of the sea, he may be terribly dangerous. And in another, just a few miles away, he may be as friendly as a puppy." She shook her head slightly at her comparison. "Or let's say, no more dangerous than any other wild creature you haven't provoked."

"Are you trying to tell me individual sharks have personalities?"

"Not specifically. I suppose what I mean is that in any given area, most of the sharks are quiet-living, law-abiding, decent members of the aquamarine society. But, for what reason we don't know, one or two of the batch may have gone bad. *They're* the ones who cause all the trouble, and the whole school gets the blackened reputation."

112

She led me over to the plate glass wall and pointed out a shark who was swimming quietly near the bottom of the pool.

"Does that one look anything like those you saw?"

I studied him. He looked to be ten or twelve feet long, but the water magnified things so I couldn't be sure. I didn't want to give him a bum rap, so I spread my hands.

Jerri indicated another one, closer to the surface. He had a dull grayish-brown back and looked bigger than the first one.

"How about our friend, *Galeocerdo cuvier?*"

"Gali-which?"

"Tiger shark to you," she said.

I studied him. Maybe it was the name he bore, maybe the intent, careful way he seemed to be studying me. His mouth gaped and I saw heavily serrated teeth slewed to one side.

"I think he's our boy," I said. "This one doesn't have any bullet holes in him, does he?"

"Not to my knowledge. You may not have hit the one you fired at, Ben. Their hides are terribly tough. If it wasn't a direct shot, it may have ricocheted off the water or even the shark himself."

I grumbled a little. Everybody was going around blithely assuming that Ben Shock cannot hit the broad side of a barn. Then I turned my attention back to the tiger shark. He came up close to the glass and returned the favor.

"Is this one special shark in captivity?" I asked. "Or do

113

you find tigers in these waters?"

"He's widely distributed in the warmer waters," Jerri Marconi said. "He likes the Gulf, but sometimes he goes up the Atlantic as far as New York. And he *is* dangerous, Ben. They've found almost everything inside tigers. Dead horses, dogs, cats, shellfish, even tin cans and pieces of outboard motor."

"So that's why Cousin Henry didn't come back from his fishing trip," I said.

We sat down again. The sun suit clung to Jerri Marconi in all the right places. It was nice to look at a pretty girl just because she *was* a pretty girl.

"How do you catch your patients?" I asked. "Me, I prefer a spinning outfit with eight pound test—"

"Not a chance," she said. "There used to be a commercial shark fishery off the coast of Florida. They kept records. One white shark is known to have broken a wire rope with a test strength of four thousand pounds. Netting's the best way. We use floaters, and lure the shark in with bait or scent. He gets caught in the net and, trying to escape, rolls it up in such a tangle that it's usually a total loss. We hoist the whole thing on board and cut him loose later."

"That's twice you've mentioned scent," I said. "Is that the yellow shark repellent stuff the navy pilots use?"

She nodded. "Except its purpose is just the opposite— to attract rather than repel." She leaned back and stretched. The effect on the sun suit's top was impressive. She saw me staring and her eyes met mine for a moment —coolly, defiantly, and not at all negatively.

114

"You see, sharks have a very well-developed sense of smell. They can identify and locate food odors from a tremendous distance. When we net them, we chum with bait fish down-current from the net, and I know for a fact, because we traced one with sonar, that they can pick up odors as far away as four or five miles. One time I soaked a weighted sack with the special scent we use and dragged it along a sandy bottom. When the sharks came in, they were just like hunting dogs on a trail—even making the same right-angle turns we'd made with the boat."

"Can they be trained? I mean, to do repetitive things, the same way seals and porpoises are?"

"Only to a limited degree. They'll respond to certain shapes and colors if used in the reward/punishment sequence."

"Which is?"

"Attach your shark's food to a certain colored paddle. He'll soon learn to come any time it's put into the water. If he comes when you use a differently colored paddle, you hit him on the nose with it and don't give him any food. In about a month, he'll respond only to the correct one."

"Could he be trained to hold a man in the water, the way poor Pritchard was held out at the tower?"

"I don't see how. Of course, a single shark, in the absence of competition, might move leisurely up to his prey, slowly gaining confidence. But the usual procedure when a pack attacks is for the first shark to anchor its teeth and shake its entire body violently to tear a chunk of flesh away. This fills the water with food scent, of course, and

115

the result is often what we call a feeding frenzy, with the pack attacking anything in the water—floating wood, boxes, bottles."

"And outboard motors," I added.

The telephone rang. She gestured toward the brandy bottle and as I poured two more healthy snifters, she answered.

"Yes, this is Jerri. Oh. I see. Of course. Yes, he's here now. Do you want to speak with him?" A pause. "All right, I'll be there." She hung up. "Ross Gautier. He wants you and me to help identify a body."

I handed her a glass. Now what the hell was my hand shaking for?

"Another so-called 'accident'?"

"No," she said, starting to turn off lights. "It's a washed-up shark." She gave me a long, appraising look. "Somebody shot it."

116

12

JAMES COPELAND was very glad to see us. Jerri had asked me to give her a lift. "I rode out with the building supervisor," she said. "He'll close up and batten down for the storm when he gets back from a trip he made to buy some cleaning supplies."

"By building manager," I said, opening the rusted door of the Nash, "you mean janitor?"

She crinkled her nose and laughed. "We don't use class-oriented titles like that any more."

I got in. "Well, if our Tour Director will stir this beast into movement, let's get downtown."

"The Old Place, Jimmy," she told him. Then, to me, "That's where Ross said to meet him."

"Blast off, James," I said, leaning back.

After a pause, she said, "I suppose Nick's broken up about Millie."

"You might put it that way," I said.

"You mean, he's drinking."

I looked at her. "You sound like you know him pretty well."

117

She tried to affect unconcern, but it's hard to hide a blush, particularly when it begins at the cheeks and radiates out like the sun rising over a pink-tinged ocean.

I looked away. "None of my business. I'm sorry."

"No," she said. "It's nothing to hide. Nick and I were close, once."

"Before or after Millie?"

She hesitated. "Both," she said. "We didn't see each other for the first year after they were married, but then—" She looked at the driver. "Well, Thomas Wolfe was right. You can't go back."

"So that's why you thought it was Nick who sicked me on you?"

"Well, it was logical. Nick used to help me out around the lab. It isn't modest, Mr. Shock, but he knows—and I know, too—that I am probably the foremost ichthyologist between here and New Orleans." Her eyes glinted. "Particularly between here and New Orleans."

I let it go by. It was obvious that Mr. Nicholas Wiggins still had a hook or two sunk in Dr. Jerri Marconi.

"Did you ever hear of any shark trouble out on the tower?" I asked.

"Nothing serious," she said. "As a matter of fact, not as much as I might have wished them."

"Aha!" I said.

"Aha, what?"

"Aha, you are one of the anti-oil ones."

"Moderately so," she admitted. "I'm a twentieth-century girl, Ben. I know we have to develop new power

118

sources. But carefully, weighing ecological balance against possible gain. Did you know they had a blowout on Offshore Two last month? It was a dry hole; otherwise this whole coast might be a dead sea today."

"Isn't that a little like the people who agree that something we need in this country is more drug treatment centers? Only for God's sake, don't build one *here!*"

She managed a smile. "Touché. But working so closely with nature, I suppose I tend to stand up for her a little too passionately."

"Somebody has to," I said. "I'm just making talk, Jerri. I guess I'm trying to avoid the question that's going to make you haul off and hit me in the nose."

Her eyes met mine again. Were they disturbed—or merely irritated by the wind?

"Ask away," she said. "I'll sit on my hands."

"You've told me that your sharks are open to the sea. They come and go pretty much as they please."

"Not quite true," she said. "Sometimes the gates are open, yes. We don't want them to develop into captive creatures."

"Doesn't it bother you, letting sharks loose that, depending on their personalities, might or might not be dangerous?"

"No," she said firmly. "We haven't imported these sharks. They were all captured locally. There's another hundred of each species swimming in the Gulf within a few miles of Cape Distress."

"All ready," I said. "Here's the big one. Jerri, isn't it

119

possible that your sharks, the ones you've been studying, might be the same ones involved in these killings?"

"Of all the stupid—" Although she had promised to sit on her hands, they started up, then she clenched them into fists and forced them into her lap. "That's the kind of ignorant, prejudiced attitude I've been fighting to overcome—"

"Down, girl," I said. "But isn't it logical? These particular sharks are around people all the time. You get right down there in the pool and swim with them. It's only natural that they may have lost some of the original fear they had of humans, and that as a result, they might be more inclined to attack."

"They haven't attacked me," she said huffily. "Not once."

"But you're very careful," I pointed out. "And you know exactly how to handle them. You're well-trained. Millie and Pritchard weren't."

"All right," she said sharply. "Our sharks *could* have been responsible. But they *weren't!*"

"How do you know?"

"I just *know,*" she said stubbornly.

I stared at her. She stared at me. Then we both broke out laughing.

"You louse," she said. "You trapped me into revealing my feminine faith-logic."

"So shoot me for a male chauvinist pig," I said.

"No," she said softly, grasping my wrist with her strong, bronzed hand. "I think I'll keep you instead."

Our driver made the turn onto Route 90 without shifting down.

"Hot dog," he yelled. "She didn't jump out!"

"Go, Mario," I said.

Jerri didn't let go of my wrist, so I slipped it around until we were holding hands. It was delightfully naughty and forbidden, and I enjoyed every minute of it.

"I'm too defensive," she said finally. "Sorry. It's just that, to draw a comparison with your drug treatment center analogy, everyone thinks it's just super that somebody's studying shark habits and behavior, but why does she have to do it in Singing River? I've been blamed for almost as many torn nets and bad fish harvests as the oil people have been blamed for everything else. We're both outcasts."

"How did you get into the shark business anyway? It's not your ordinary high school major."

"On my tenth birthday, my daddy gave me a bowl of goldfish."

"And *that* started you?"

"They died because I filled the bowl with salt water. I hated myself. Then I started trying to learn about fish. When I thought I knew enough, I saved up my allowance and went down to the five and dime and bought two more goldfish. They died, too. That *really* made me mad. I devoured everything the library had about fish. I wrote to the Department of Agriculture. I even made phone calls to those radio shows that talk back and forth with listeners. Somewhere along the way, I picked up enough information so that when I got my next pair of goldfish they lived. As long as goldfish normally live, anyway. By the time they passed on, I had so many fish of all kinds that I didn't even miss them."

"Florence Nightingale of the sea," I said.

"Sounds that way, doesn't it? How about you, Ben? Were you always a cop?"

"Only since I've been twelve," I said. "Before that I was a sheriff when I wasn't being The Lone Ranger. I tried a summer as Tonto, but all those keemosaves got to me."

"Seriously."

"Seriously? My family's been in blue since my grandfather, who came over from Ireland and discovered he didn't like being a second-class citizen in a first-class country. But instead of attacking the system and trying to tear it down, he joined it and tried to make it better."

"Do I detect a slight tinge of anti-revolutionary bias there?"

"Bias is when I don't agree with *your* bias. I prefer to call it basic self-preservation, a term which has, I agree, fallen into disrepute. We aren't supposed to care what happens to us or those we love today. Instead, we're required to suffer for the underprivileged, the undereducated, the undermotivated, the underhonest. Somehow their failure is all *our* fault. Well, I don't buy that. I agree that there's a lot wrong with our world, but blowing it up isn't going to improve things for anybody. Pipe bombs in post offices just delay everybody's mail and kill

122

innocent people who didn't even know they were in a war. I'm sorry that a small percentage of this country's citizens have been badly treated, and I hope to see the day when such things can't occur. Meanwhile, I'm bound to resist any efforts of the radicals, the Weathermen, the black extremists, the KKK's, the religious fanatics, or even the American Indians to burn down my part of the house because they don't like their own."

Slowly, she said, "Where's the answer then?"

I shrugged. "My answer is to go on doing the best I can, not kicking anybody in the head unless I absolutely have to, and keeping my ass down when the shooting starts."

"May you live in interesting times," she said.

"What's that?"

"An ancient Chinese curse."

"Very clever, those Chinese," I said.

The car trembled under a sudden gust of wind. Copeland almost lost it. We went over the double yellow line. An approaching truck blasted an air horn at us. Copeland veered back into the right lane.

"Hilda's starting to blow up real good," he said.

"Maybe you ought to let her slip down into second," I said.

"Oh, don't you worry none," he said. "No sir, I got this car right in line now. That first gust just sort of surprised me."

We passed another car nosed down into a roadside ditch.

"We may be in for it this time," Jerri Marconi said.

I looked back at the car in the ditch. "You may be right."

"Shouldn't we stop?" she asked.

Copeland jerked his head toward the rear-view mirror. "Nobody hurt," he said. "Driver already got out and he's walking up to that house to phone for the wrecker. Checked that right off."

I saw that he was right. Okay, this wasn't the New York State Thruway. Maybe people *would* stop if you were in trouble. I was glad to find out that I'd been wrong about James Copeland.

We turned off into the road leading to The Old Place. As we passed the Baptist cemetery, I saw two gravediggers working, building up a heap of red earth.

Jerri stared. "Is that for Millie?" she asked.

"I don't know," I said. "Probably not."

"Oh, yes sir," said good old Copeland. "They're going to have the funeral right away."

Angrily, I said, "How the hell do you know so much?"

Calmly, he answered, "My brother Cecil's the undertaker. He hired me and my cousin Benny for pallbearers."

"What the hell's the hurry?"

"Can't blame Miss Lisa," he said. "If we don't beat this storm, it might hold proceedings up four, five days. Even more, if there's bad damage. Those delays are mighty hard on a family, I can tell you. Hey, I should have known. You're that detective feller from New York, ain't you?

Driving a big black Cadillac Fleetwood with a souped-up engine under the hood?"

I wanted to shut him up, but automotive pride came to the fore.

"What makes you think it isn't factory-equipped?" I said.

"I saw you slipping through town last night. Saw the car, that is. Couldn't see your face, or I'd of known you today. Got a good look at the car though. Later on, while you all was inside, the Dantzlers' yardman moved your car into the garage. Told me that when he let out on the clutch, that motor nearly snapped his head off. Said the hood was locked, but that he'd bet there was twin carbs in there and overhead cams, too."

"The yardman has a big mouth," I said.

"Oh, it don't matter him talking to me," said Copeland. "He's my nephew, on my wife's side."

"Is there anybody in Singing River you aren't related to?" I growled.

"Ain't related to you," he said. "Or Miss Marconi here, beg your pardon, ma'am. No wop blood on either side of my family, far as I know. Wait a minute; that's not so. We do have one in the family, kind of distant, though."

"Tell me it's a guy named Bellavia who runs a fishing camp," I said. "That'll make my day."

"Glad to hear it," he said, pulling up in front of The Old Place. "Because that's just who it is. Married my third cousin on my mother's side."

125

Jerri Marconi leaned forward. "Jimmy," she said sweetly, "will you do something for me?"

"Sure thing, ma'am," he said. "Anything in the world."

She patted his shoulder. "Shut your fat lip."

He choked. But he shut his fat lip.

13

I RANG the doorbell. It was answered almost instantly.

Margaret nodded. "Come on in, Mr. Shock. Miss Marconi, nice to see you again."

As Jerri followed Margaret inside, I went back to Number Two and dug in my pocket for the wad of bills. "How much I owe you?"

Copeland hesitated. "I sure didn't mean to stir you folks up. Reckon I talk too much. Why don't we call this one even, a kind of Welcome to Singing River present?"

"Bull," I said. I peeled off a ten. "That okay?"

He shook his head. "Too much. Too much even for a tourist, and I see now I was sure wrong to take you for a tourist. Make it five even, and I'm still ahead."

I found a five and gave it to him. He turned the key.

"Hey, Jim," I said.

"Yes sir?"

"You put just a little transmission fluid in that gear box the next time you lube up and I bet she'll stay in third."

He grinned and shook his head. "No way in the world,

Mr. Shock. That box is plumb full of sawdust right now."

I shuddered and waved good-by.

Inside, the group gathered around the dining room table looked like a modern version of The Last Supper. Lisa Dantzler was at the head, sipping coffee. Charity sat next to her, and beside my girl was Nick Wiggins. He wore a black mourning band on his sleeve. Somehow it didn't look corny.

Margaret was ushering Jerri to a chair. I heard Nick introducing her to Charity.

My girl looked at me. I felt an insane urge to rub my cheek to see if there was lipstick there. Instead, I made a little dabbling wave with five fingers of my left hand.

There wasn't any sign of the old man Charity and I had seen upstairs last night.

"Howdy, Ben," said a voice behind me. I turned. It was Ross Gautier.

"Chief."

"Dr. Marconi give you any new information?"

"Some," I said. Then, watching his face, "You didn't tell me she wasn't a man."

"Didn't feel it necessary," he said, smiling. "You didn't have any trouble seeing the difference, did you?"

"Bastard," I said under my breath. "If I'd known she was a beach bunny, I would have taken a chaperon."

"You don't mean to say that you got apron strings hitched up to you, Ben?" he said, chuckling wickedly.

He looked over my shoulder at Charity, then back at me. "Come to think of it, appears you do." He chuckled

128

again. "Why, I'm sure sorry to stir up any trouble between you and Miss Tucker."

"Okay, Ross," I said. "Cut the comedy. What's the big idea?"

His smile vanished. "On the level, Ben. I wanted you to go out there without any preconceived notions about our Dr. Marconi. You see things pretty straight. You think she's mixed up in this mess?"

"Directly? No."

"How about indirectly?"

I gave a little nod toward Nick Wiggins. "Him."

"Let's us go outside," said Gautier. He led the way toward the back door. We left without saying anything to those at the table.

The circular pool was drained. Its bottom was littered with wet algae and pine needles.

Gautier offered me a cigarette. It was a Pall Mall, so I accepted with a nod. The hell with those menthol sticks Charity smokes.

We lit up. The Surgeon General in far-off Washington made two more marks on his table of statistics. Screw him. They say that just breathing the air in our nation's capital is the same as smoking three packs a day.

"What about Wiggins?" asked Gautier.

"You knew he was mixed up with the Marconi broad."

"Sure I did. Everybody knew it. Everybody except Millie."

"Lisa, too?"

"Lisa most of all. More than once, Lisa was the beard."

129

I stared at him. Chief Ross Gautier of Singing River, Mississippi, couldn't be *that* hip.

He was. "That's what I said, Ben. Lisa and her friend, Jerri Marconi, would go out for dinner. Or a pizza. Or a movie. Or maybe one of those fancier shows over in Gulfport, where them stripteasers show you everything they got and practically let you lean over and taste it, too. God's truth, Ben, I never thought I'd see the day when them places was wide open, let alone now when there's almost as many women watching as there are men."

"And our friend Nick would accidentally run into the girls and join them, pretending he was just being a good brother-in-law."

"You can't miss action like that in a small town, Ben."

"Why?"

He shrugged. "You got to admit Jerri's a good-looking girl."

"But I'd swear she's a straight one, too."

"Not so straight she didn't have two affairs with Nick Wiggins. The first, before he was married, nobody could fault. Hell, some of the best marriages on the shore started out that way. But after he'd been married to Millie for a little more'n a year, it started up again. That was a different story, but none of my business. I'd never have given it a second thought if it wasn't for the way Miss Lisa was helping it along."

"No chance she was an innocent dupe?"

"She let them use her car more than once because Nick's is so well-known."

130

"All right," I said, wondering at a slight sinking sensation in my stomach. What did I care if Jerri Marconi had been banging Nick Wiggins in every motel in Mississippi? "What do you figure? Nick picking Jerri's brain to find a way to murder Millie without risk? With sharks?"

"Nope," said Gautier. "I admit, that was a mighty tempting route to take, though. But there's one thing that shuts it off."

"What?"

"Nick wouldn't have conspired, with or without Jerri's knowledge, to murder his wife just so he could have Jerri. Ben, don't think too badly of Millie. You know how it is with boys and girls. You get the chemistry right and there's no accounting for good sense. Nick could make her do anything he wanted just by a wave of his little finger. So he didn't need to get rid of Millie. He could have his cake and eat it, too."

"Maybe he also wanted to own a chunk of an oil well."

Gautier shook his head. "That's why I've eliminated Nick from my list. Ben, he doesn't get a thing. Not dollar one."

"You mean Millie disinherited him?"

"He wasn't ever inherited. Oh, I don't know the little ins and outs of inheritance law here. Maybe he gets to keep the car and the house, but they ain't all that much. As for Dantzler Oil, neither she nor Lisa can leave it to anyone else as long as the other sister lives. They had reciprocal wills, drawn in such a way as to eliminate dower rights, if a man even has such rights. But even if he contested the wills, it wouldn't do any good, because the actual vested interest in the company is tied up in a trust that doesn't dissolve until *both* sisters are dead."

"Beautiful," I said. "And who thought up that Chinese puzzle?"

"Old man Dantzler," said the Chief. "He wasn't anybody's fool. He saw the possibility of sharpies moving in on his little girls when he was gone. There wasn't any male heir to pass things along to. So he did the best he could for his daughters. They'd both have all the income and the control of the company, but its ownership passes, on the death of the last surviving sister—get this, Ben—to the Pima Indian Nation."

"You've got to be kidding," I said. "You mean the only ones who will benefit if both girls get killed are the redskins?"

"That's the story."

"I should have tried being Tonto longer," I mumbled.

"So, since he's in no way part Pima Indian, there's not a dime in it for Nick Wiggins," said Gautier.

"Or anybody else," I said glumly. "We seem to have that most delicious of crimes, the one without a motive."

"We're not even sure there's been a crime, Ben," he pointed out.

"Sorry. What's this about a shark?"

"We found one washed up by the breakwater."

"How the hell am I supposed to identify a shark?"

He shrugged. "Between you and Jerri, maybe we can find out if there's any connection. I've got a man probing

132

for bullets, but he said as far as he can see, only one hit and it went all the way through."

"I was in the pool with that goddamned shark," I said. "I had to have hit him more than once."

"One time," he said thoughtfully, "I was sitting on watch during a deer hunt up in northern Louisiana. We used dogs then, and I heard them all around my stand. Pretty soon, I looked up and there, less than ten feet in front of me, was the most beautiful ten-point buck you ever laid eyes on. I slipped my gun up, rested it on a *tree*, by God, and squeezed off. I emptied the magazine, five shots. And I didn't hit that deer one single time."

"All that proves," I said, "is that you're subject to buck fever and I'm not."

He smiled. "But there's always *shark* fever, city boy." He waved a deputy over. "Pete, we're going over by the breakwater where the shark was found. Would you bring Dr. Marconi down?"

"Will do," said the deputy.

As we strolled through the ankle-deep sand, I said, "Why the Pima Indians, Ross?"

"Dantzler screwed them out of some water rights years ago," Gautier said. "I guess this was his way of making up for it."

I paused in mid-stride, hesitated, then kept walking.

"What?" said Gautier.

"It's too crazy," I said.

"You mean, could someone from the Pima nation be trying to hustle up the delivery of that trust?"

"Something like that."

"We raised that thought," he said, leading me around an old concrete structure. I looked at it. He indicated it with one hand. "Gun emplacement, left over from World War Two. We had artillery all up and down the coast then. This was torpedo alley. Wasn't a morning, when I was a kid, you couldn't come down on the beach and find bananas and other cargo washed up on the shore." He spat. "Bodies, too. We had a dim-out like you wouldn't believe. Car headlights were masked down with tape so there was only an inch-wide strip left open. Blackout curtains on all the beach homes. Didn't make a damned bit of difference. You could go out two, three in the morning and see the ships burning out there. The war came real close, here. Most people don't realize it."

We climbed over a two-foot-high concrete barrier. It was an old sea wall. Beyond it, down at the edge of the dry sand, a man crouched over a large object.

It was a dead shark. And beginning to stink. August is not a good month for dead sharks.

Gautier waved at the shark. "What about it?"

I examined the huge body, flattened against the sand. Flies were buzzing around it. The deputy who had been probing with a sharp hunting knife had doused the shark down with salt water, but it didn't help much. A dead shark is *ripe,* and there's not much else to be said.

"I can't say," I told him. "Listen, Ross, all I saw of that bastard were teeth and fins. I'd be lying if I claimed I could say that this one was or wasn't the one in the pool."

134

"Any guess on the caliber of the bullet, Harry?" asked Gautier.

The deputy shook his head. "Salt water rots out a wound real quick," he said. "Hell, it could have been a mortar shell and I couldn't swear to it."

"You guys are a lot of help," grumbled Gautier. "Why the hell don't sharks leave fingerprints?"

Jerri Marconi came over the sea wall. She stared down at the dead shark. "Oh," she said. "Oh."

"Dr. Marconi," Gautier said formally, "I know this is unusual, but we're stumped. Is there any way you could tell if this is one of the sharks you've been working with?"

She stared at the stinking body. She shook her head. "I'd know," she said. "If I were unsure, I'd go back to the lab and check my photos. But I'm positive. This shark has never been inside my lab. He's a wild one."

"What was he doing in that swimming pool then?" asked Gautier.

"I don't know."

"Look again," he said.

"I've looked!" she flared. "I wouldn't lie. If it were one of my sharks, I'd tell you. It isn't." She turned to me. "Is this the one you shot, Ben?"

"I don't know," I said.

"This is a requiem shark," she told me. "If there's a killer around here, this tiger shark is the most likely species."

"Which is he?" asked Ross Gautier. "A requiem or a tiger?"

"Both," she said. "Any man-eater is called a requiem."

"Good name," he said shortly. "But you ain't never seen him before?"

"No."

"I guess I got to accept your word."

"Thank you," she said. "Ben, I wish you luck. I think I'd better go back to the house and call the lab. I want to make sure they're closing up for the storm."

"Are we through here, Chief?" I asked Gautier.

"You and Dr. Marconi are," he said. "We've got to examine this shark a little more."

"I thought you couldn't tell what kind of bullet went through him."

"We can't," he said. "But if this bastard chewed up Millie Wiggins, there'll be part of her in his stomach."

"Sorry I asked," I said, helping Jerri Marconi over the sea wall.

"You've hit us at a bad time, Ben," she said as we walked up to the house. "Violent death, a hurricane brewing out in the Gulf, humidity that would melt a marble statue. You must not think much of Mississippi."

"I've seen it hotter," I said. "And I've seen them deader. No, Jerri, I'm not down on your state. The truth is, I haven't seen enough of it to say one way or the other."

"Maybe we can rectify that," she said, looking at me.

"I hope so," I said. Our eyes were locked together like two pairs of handcuffs. I turned away first.

At the house, I said, "You go on in. I want to get something out of my car."

"Then I'll see you later?" she asked.

I hesitated. "Later," I said finally.

She went into the house. I headed for the garage, under the round white lighthouse. Inside, I opened the glove compartment and took out the folding Philippine fighting knife I'd been given by a buddy in Vietnam. I tucked it down inside one of my socks under the trouser leg. Now I didn't feel quite so naked.

There was a door leading out of the side of the garage. I assumed it went toward the house, and opened it.

It didn't. Instead, it led to a spiral staircase that wound up into the gloom of the lighthouse's interior.

What the hell? I'd never been inside a lighthouse before. I went in and started up the stairs.

Halfway to the top, I heard a sound.

It was Charity's voice saying, "Be careful with that bayonet."

I looked around. Had she seen me tuck the fighting knife into my sock?

But she was far above me, in the top of the lighthouse. She spoke again. "Careful!"

I went up the stairs as fast as I could. Running around in circles like that could make you dizzy. But I got to the top all right, puffing from lack of wind. The winding staircase opened into a large room surrounded by glass windows. In its center was a huge arrangement of mirrors and spotlights.

Charity was backed up against it. In front of her was the old man we'd seen at the end of the hall.

137

He held a rifle, and on its end was a long, shining bayonet. He had its point pressed against my girl's throat.

I slipped up behind him, reached out with one hand, caught the stock of the rifle and pulled it away from Charity. With the other arm, I circled the old man's neck and pressed him up against me.

"You move, old man," I promised, "and I'll break your scrawny neck!"

He choked something, and Charity straightened. "No, Ben," she said. "Don't hurt him. It isn't what you think."

I tossed the rifle over onto a table and turned the old man around. "What the hell's going on?" I asked.

Charity pushed her way between us. "Let him go, you big bully. This is Uncle Edgar Dantzler. He's a friend of mine. He's just been showing me how they were trained to use bayonets in the Great War."

Sourly, I said, "Which Great War was that?"

"The War to End Wars," croaked the old man. He rubbed his neck. "Son, you got a mean grip on you there."

Charity gripped my arm. "Uncle Edgar and I were just talking about his hobbies." Her eyes pleaded with me to go along with her. "He's an expert on bayonets. He collects them, all shapes and sizes."

"Good for him," I said, still shaking. "Then he goes out and practices on visiting tourists who are stupid enough to go up in an abandoned lighthouse with him?"

"Shush," said Charity. "Uncle Edgar's usually either working on his collection or looking out the windows here. He can see for miles. All the way out to Ship Island on a clear day. Or at night, he can look straight down at the swimming pool."

"How about that," I said. "Where did you learn to use these pig-stickers, Uncle Edgar?"

"I served with Black Jack Pershing," he said proudly. "We didn't hide out in those trenches, no sir. Over the top and down with the Hun."

"That's the way to do it."

"I never lost the knack," he said. "Why, I could peel a peach with that there bayonet and never lose a drop of juice. One time, I speared me a shark right between the eyes, and he just floated belly up and never twitched a muscle. That's a mean weapon, son."

"I believe you," I said. "Do you hunt sharks often?"

"I don't go out of my way looking for them," he said. "But I don't run from one neither."

"When's the last time you saw one?"

He started to speak, then shook his head. "Don't recollect," he said. "You got so many of those bastards around here, you can't hardly go fishing without running into one or two."

"Where do you fish?"

"Up and down the coast."

"Do you ever go out of Bellavia's camp on the river?"

The old man looked away. "I got to get me my supper," he said. "What did you do with my Springfield? That's a genuine Army of Northern Virginia bayonet on there. I wouldn't want to lose it."

I handed him the rifle. The bolt was welded shut. Somebody had already made sure that Uncle Edgar's reenactments of history would be limited to cold steel.

Charity took my arm. "We'll be down in a while, Uncle Edgar," she said.

"Suit yourself," he said, and left.

I heard his feet shuffling down the circular staircase for what seemed an hour. Then all was silent. I looked at Charity and shook my head.

"What are you using for brains these days?" I asked.

"Oh, he's harmless."

"Are you sure of that?" I touched her throat. There was a tiny fleck of blood where the bayonet had opened the skin.

Charity has read her tactics. When in danger, attack. She said, "Who's the blonde?"

"The blonde is Dr. Jerri Marconi of the Cape Distress Shark Research Laboratory."

"Too bad about her broken leg."

"*What* broken leg?"

"I saw you helping her over that little sea wall. You never help *me* over sea walls. I assumed she was crippled."

"Ho, ho," I said. "Listen, baby, let's cut the Bette Davis dialogue."

A trace of a smile flicked at her lips. "Only if you try to forget you're Mike Hammer."

I kissed her. She stiffened, but then she kissed back. It was nice. Almost like in the movies.

She pulled away. "What did the crippled blonde tell you?"

140

"That there are killer sharks in these waters. They call them requiem sharks. But she's never heard of one turning up in a swimming pool before."

Charity stepped over to the window and looked almost straight down at the circular pool beside the house. "But one did," she said.

"What did you find out from your buddy on WWL?"

"Mostly, he steered me to other people who would talk. Not very much, actually. As you've probably guessed, it's common knowledge that Ross Gautier is that rare breed, an honest cop."

"So tell me something new."

"Your friend Grover Ellis doesn't have the same reputation. It's widely believed that he is a no-good skunk who would steal your wallet, your car, your woman or your life, depending on which appealed to him at the moment. But he's never been caught at it yet."

"That's a surprise to me," I grumbled.

"So? Sometimes appearances *aren't* deceiving, Ben."

"What about your Miss Lisa?"

"Since when is she my Miss Lisa?"

"Since that magic telephone of yours got out of line and faked us into this deal in the first place."

"According to the gossip, Lisa's played around here and there. And with this and that."

"Which is what and what?"

"Pot and hash and other assorted goodies. Again, no proof. Just a liberated twentieth-century woman who owns her own thoughts and body."

"Isn't that the motto of *Ms. Magazine?*"

"Pig."

"Sow."

She slapped me. I slapped her back.

"Hey," she said. "I was only joking."

"So was I," I said.

"You hurt."

"So did you."

"I meant to."

My knuckles were stinging slightly. I wet them with my lips. "I didn't. I'm sorry, Charity. It was just a reflex action."

She took my hand and kissed it. "I know. Me, too. It was reflex to strike out at you because I hate seeing you snuggling up so close to layable blondes."

"Ah sees, Counselor Tucker. And who does you represent, the lay*or* or the lay*ee?*"

"She's got quite a reputation, your Dr. Marconi."

"You mean her and Nick Wiggins?"

"How did you know?"

"A little bird."

"Did the same little bird tell you that Lawyer Wiggins was once investigated by the state bar association for a little deal that smelled faintly rotten?"

"No."

"Maybe it's unimportant. He was cleared. Something about misplacing a few thousand dollars of a trust fund. He convinced the bar association it was an honest error— which, to be fair, it may have been."

"Where is Nick now?"

"Over at the undertaker's parlor." She grimaced. "Ugh. What a name. Anyway, he's making all the arrangements. They're trying to hold the funeral tomorrow morning in hopes of beating the hurricane."

"I know."

"You seem to know a lot, Shock. I thought *I* was doing all the undercover checking. Where have *you* been?"

"Riding in an old Nash that you would have to see to believe. It is piloted by a gentleman with a well-lubricated mouth."

She looked at her watch. "Oh-oh, I'm late. I have an appointment downtown to talk to a gabby lady who once wrote the Singing River gossip column for the Pascagoula *Chronicle-Star.*"

"I'll drop you," I said. "I want to check up on Bellavia's Fishing Camp. Too many people keep dropping that name around."

We circled our way down the stairs. I opened the car door and she got in.

"Thank you, sir," she said. "We'll make a gentleman out of you yet, Jerri Marconi and I."

"Keep picking at it," I said. "Maybe it'll start to bleed."

Charity hunched down in the seat. "I think it already has."

She didn't say another word as we drove down to Route 90 and turned toward Singing River. I let her off at Courthouse Square and circled around to head east toward the river and the fishing camp.

143

14

I MISSED the turnoff the first time and found myself heading into Pascagoula. I turned around and went back. Then I saw the sign, faded and peeling: BELLAVIA'S FISHING CAMP. *Bait, Boats, Motors.* I turned left off Route 90, drove down toward the beach. Another sign directed me to turn into a pine-shaded area that looked like the old-fashioned tourist cabins of the thirties.

The buildings were white stucco, neat and well-cared-for. There wasn't any litter on the grounds, and the road-way was neatly marked with white stones. A larger building crouched near the water's edge. I parked near a sign that said BOAT LAUNCH $1.00.

A slim man in his late fifties came out and nodded at me. "Howdy," he said. "Sorry, we're all booked up."

"Maybe next time," I said. "I'm looking for Mr. Bellavia."

He stuck out his hand. "That's me. Fred." He looked at the New York license plates on the Fleetwood. "Passing through?"

"I'm doing a little work for some folks over in Singing River," I said. "You got a minute to talk?"

"Come on inside," he said. "It's air-conditioned. And I've got some cold beer, if you're so inclined."

"I'm inclined," I said, following him.

The beer was Falstaff, and it was so cold it hurt my teeth. I endured the pain and put one can down in record time, reached for a second. It was just as good. I nodded at Bellavia. "That's good medicine."

"In moderation," he said. "What can I do for you? You're not that feller who's investigating for the Dantzler Oil people, are you? A Mr. Ben Shock?"

"I am," I said. "It's sure hard to keep a secret down here."

He laughed. "Oh, word gets around. Used to be, you could get a message from Biloxi to Mobile quicker by telling it to one of the men down at the Louisville and Nashville station and swearing him to secrecy than you could by putting it on the telegraph wire. But times are changing. It's just that I get a lot of business from the Dantzler oilmen, and one of them mentioned you."

"And went on to describe me and my car?"

"No, I got those two facts from a relative—"

"Don't tell me. A displaced fighter pilot named Copeland."

He bobbed his head. "None other. Said you seemed to be a good old boy."

I dug out a couple of dollar bills. "Let me pay for those

beers and buy you one," I said.

He shook his head. "Those first ones was on me. I invited you."

"Now I'm inviting you, then."

He wet his lips and grinned. "Well, it's a little early in the day for me, but I reckon I could choke one down." He popped open two more cans of Falstaff. "That'll be fifty cents."

I stared at him. "A *quarter* a beer?"

He looked troubled. "Well, I can't hardly sell them no cheaper. They cost me—"

"No, no," I said. "I'm not complaining. It's just that I'm used to paying seventy-five cents."

"For *one* beer?" I nodded and he shook his head. "Mr. Shock, somebody is counting your money for you."

"I'm beginning to think you're right." I toasted with the can. "Good luck."

"Same to you." He sipped. "Well, what did you want to ask me?"

"You had a fairly regular guest, a man named Guy Pritchard."

"Rest his soul," agreed Fred Bellavia. "Quiet feller, stuck to hisself. Maybe drank a little too much. I used to cart a wheelbarrow full of beer cans away from his cabin when he'd been here a few days. But he never caused any trouble."

"He saw something here," I said. "I think it's what got him killed."

Bellavia hesitated. "I heard that was an accident. He fell

146

in the water and a shark got him."

"I think he might have been pushed. I'm trying to find out why."

Bellavia thought for a moment. "There's been nothing happening out here that he was involved in that I can remember. He just came for four, five days, rented a boat and motor and fished. Gave all his catch to the boy that cleans up for me. Once or twice, he come in and had a few beers, but mostly he stayed in his cabin."

"Which one was that?"

"Mostly Number Two. Since he always came ashore on a Thursday, the weekly guests were moving out that day and he had his pick. He always picked Two, when it was available, which was most of the time."

"Any reason?"

"It's away from the bigger ones, where the families stay with their kids. Maybe quieter. And it's got a nice view of the river."

"Where is it?"

He pointed out a white building. It was set back in the pines, near another one between it and the water.

"If he wanted a view, why didn't he take that other one?"

"Number One? Oh, that's been booked up for the whole season. Some Galveston men."

"Dantzler people?"

"No, I don't think so. They ain't here much, but they don't seem to keep regular tours of work like those tower oilmen do."

"Did Pritchard have anything to do with them? I mean, pal around or go out honky-tonking or that kind of thing?"

"Not that I know of. Like I said, he kept pretty much to himself. I hear he was married. That's too bad. Those oil boys, they don't usually carry much insurance. Premiums come too high."

"Did you notice anything unusual about the men in Cabin One?"

Bellavia hesitated. "Well, they never caused any trouble either. They've got their own boat, a nice thirty-foot Chris Craft. You could go to Cuba in that without thinking twice. But one thing always puzzled me. I know they may be using artificial lures, but in all the time they been here, they've never bought one ounce of live bait from me—and as far as I know, they ain't never brought in a single fish either."

"Are you sure about that?"

"Not unless they snuck in after dark and hid it. I'm tied up with the state conservation folks, and they like me to kind of keep a check on what comes in from the Gulf. There ain't no limits or anything, but they want to get an idea of how much fishing pressure there really is. So I watch out, when it don't interfere with my regular work, and I could swear those four boys in Cabin One never caught a fish yet, unless they released him back overboard."

I had a momentary vision of good old Ben striking oil, an image that fitted my present client.

"Are they there now?" I asked.

"Nope. Went off this morning."

"Any chance of me looking around in there?"

"You carry any tin?"

I shook my head. "I used to, but I travel without a badge now."

"Sorry then," he said. "You know how it is."

"Sure," I said.

"Copeland tells me you and Ross Gautier are real buddy-buddy," he commented.

"We seem to get along."

He finished his beer. "Well, I've got to run out in the bay and check my shrimp traps. If you're still around when those boys in Number One show up, their key's right there, behind the cash register. Nice meeting you, Ben. I reckon I'll be gone an hour or so."

"So long," I said. I watched him walk slowly down to the end of the wharf, step aboard a small boat, start the engine, and nose out into the channel.

Maybe he hadn't meant it to be an invitation, but I was willing to accept it that way. I took the key to Cabin One off its hook and dropped it in my pocket.

The wind was gusting heavily as I walked across the driveway. Fred Bellavia was probably getting wet.

The door opened easily and I went in.

I assumed Bellavia must furnish maid service. The cabin was too neat for four guys batching it together. It only took a few minutes to check all the usual hiding places: inside the toilet tank, the back sides of the dresser drawers, behind hanging pictures. Nothing.

Several fishing rods were piled in one corner. As much because I am a hopelessly addicted fisherman as for any other reason, I examined them.

It was as odd an assortment of gear as you'd find anywhere in the world. Little featherweight rods burdened with a star-drag Double O reel and eighty-pound test monofilament. And just the opposite, a light spinning reel and ten-pound test on a surf rod that should have been carrying tackle five times that weight.

Whoever the boys from Galveston were, they weren't fishermen. The line was all brand-new and obviously hadn't been unwound since it had been put on the reels.

Now, why would four men go out burdened with fishing rods they never used? If they just wanted to boat, they didn't need the fishing props.

I heard a footstep behind me.

Ben Shock, boy burglar, was trapped.

Slowly, I turned.

15

THERE WERE two of them. They seemed more puzzled than angry to find me in their cabin.

"Who are you?" asked one, the taller. He wore rough green work pants and a plaid shirt. His buddy, a runt of only five feet or so, was all spiffed up in a blue nylon windbreaker and pegged trousers. They both had grocery bags in their hands.

"Afternoon," I said. "I think Fred gave me the wrong key. These rods yours?"

"Sure they're ours," said Shorty.

"Nice equipment," I said.

"We like it," said the taller man. "How come you got our key?"

"Some kind of mixup," I said. "I rented a cabin for a couple of days and Fred said the key was behind the cash register. This was the only one I saw, but he must have meant for me to take the cabin next door, unless you boys are moving out."

"We ain't moving anywhere," said Shorty. "We paid rent on this shack for the whole summer."

"Here, let me help you," I said, taking one of the paper bags from him and putting it on the table. It was full of canned goods and cold cuts. "I've got to buy some grub, too. Where's the nearest store?"

Despite himself, Shorty responded to my helpfulness. "There's one just up Route 90, but stay out of it. It's a trap. Go on down to the Piggly-Wiggly market. It's cheaper."

"Thanks," I said, holding out the key. "Sorry about the mixup. Can I buy you boys a beer?"

"I thought Fred was gone."

"Oh, I just put the money in the cash register."

"You must know Fred pretty well," said the tall man.

"Off and on. I've been up north working for the past year or so." Which was true, as far as it went.

"We got some beer here," said the tall man. He took a six-pack of Jax out of one of the bags and popped three and passed them around. "I'm Jesse, this here's Hodge."

"Ben."

"You in oil, Ben?"

I laughed. "No way. I sell storm windows."

Jesse laughed. "Hear tell that's not the straightest racket in the world."

I shrugged. "I just sell them. If the mark—the customer —doesn't get exactly what he thought he'd get, that's no skin off my nose. I'm in the next town by then."

The Jax tasted bitter after the Falstaff. And full of bubbles. I burped.

152

"How long are you going to be around, Ben?" asked the short one, Hodge.

"Two, three days."

"Storm coming up," said Jesse. "You don't want to fool around out there in a small boat."

"I know," I said. "Just my luck. Fellow over in Mobile told me they'd put up a Texas Tower out there somewhere. You can get awful good fishing around them for some reason. But it's probably out too far to risk it until the storm blows over."

"Too far for a small boat anyway," said Hodge. "It's out of sight of land. Get turned around and you'd find yourself on the way to Tampa."

"I'd use a compass," I said.

The two men didn't like the way this conversation was going. I decided to get out of there while we were still friendly. The mention of Bugs Bunny had tightened their smiles.

I put down the half-empty can. "Well, I better get down to that supermarket before it closes."

"We'll be seeing you," said Hodge, making no attempt to keep me there.

See? Clever Ben, always able to talk his way out of a tight spot.

The door opened again and in came two more men.

One looked at me and said, "That's him."

"So long," I said, trying to brush past them.

It didn't work. They grabbed me. I might have been

153

able to work my mysterious judo tricks on them and escape into the driveway, but it would have been hard to outrun a bullet from the ugly black .45 automatic Hodge had produced from inside his windbreaker, so I didn't move. Instead, I said, "I don't believe it. I'm going to get mugged in Singing River, Mississippi."

"Search him," said one of the men holding me.

Hodge's buddy Jesse got my wallet and some postcards I'd bought up in Alabama planning to write on for my friends in New York. He rummaged through my ID.

"Ben Shock," he said. "He told us his name was Ben."

One of the men holding me swore. "He *told* you that and you gave him a beer? This is that private cop the Dantzlers hired. Where were you when they passed out the brains, behind the door?"

Jesse said, "He told us he was a storm window salesman."

"Beautiful," said one of my captors, pushing me inside and closing the door. "And what did you tell him? Your name, rank, and serial number?"

Hodge moved back, keeping the pistol trained on my stomach. He licked his lips nervously. "He knows our names," he said. "And he was asking a lot of questions about the tower."

"Well, shut your yap before he knows everything else, too," said the man. "Is he packing any iron?"

"I didn't feel any," said Jesse.

"Check again."

Jesse patted me down good this time. But he missed the

154

knife in my sock—which is why I carry it there.

"He's clean," Jesse said.

"Let's get him out to the boat," said the man.

They started to turn me toward the door, and that's when I made my break. I kicked out with one foot and caught someone on the ankle. He bellowed in pain and rage. I dove out the half-open door, hit the ground rolling to my feet. If I could only get a head start, I didn't think they'd risk using a pistol in this public place.

I was wrong. Hodge squeezed off a shot that fanned my cheek with its passage. That wasn't any warning round. He'd been trying to hit me. I got my arms up in the air fast. I didn't know what they had in store for me, but anything was better than being knocked down by a .45 slug.

Now they roughed me up a little as they hustled me toward the wharf. I hoped someone would stick his head out of a cabin to investigate the shot. But nobody did.

Their boat was a low-profiled cruiser. Roughly, Jesse shoved me sprawling into the cockpit. Hodge jumped in after me.

"Take care of him," said the other man, one of the two left on the dock. "We'd better get our stuff out of here in case there's any heat about that shot."

"Don't worry," said Jesse. He put his foot in the small of my back and stood up. A wave of pain and nausea swept over me. "Be a nice boy now and don't move, you hear? Or I'll break your backbone for you."

The engine throbbed and the boat moved away from the

155

pier. The water was choppy. I smelled oil and gasoline fumes and they made me sicker.

Distantly, I heard Hodge's voice say, "Tie him up and stick his wallet back in his pocket."

"Throw me a rope," said Jesse.

Something hit me on the back of the neck. It was wet and cold and felt like a coiled snake.

Jesse had tied folks up before. He made a loop around my neck, then bound my hands, and finally fastened the other end of the rope around my ankles. If I moved around, I would choke myself to death.

I'd tried the old routine of tensing my muscles so I would have some slack to work with. But Jesse stole that away from me by kicking me in the side just as he made the knots, and when he finished, I couldn't wiggle a finger. My hands were clasped around the calves of my legs, leaving me in the approximate configuration of a pretzel.

The Chris Craft hit heavier seas.

"That storm's on her way in," Hodge said. "I don't want to take this boat outside."

"You don't have to," said Jesse. "Just get out far enough to pick up the channel. We don't want him washing ashore around here."

That wasn't the surprise I thought it would be. My friends had a little ducking in mind for me. Tied as I was, it would be a brief one. Once the air in my lungs was gone, that would be it.

Well, it comes for all of us. And it is always too soon. It is always a mistake. Not *me,* the stunned mind replies

156

when its name is called, no matter how many countless millions have answered the summons before.

My father once told me of a double execution he witnessed at Sing Sing. A woman had enlisted her paramour to help in the murder of her husband and her three children. All through the trial and the round of appeals, the two remained obstinate in the justice of what they had done. Theirs was the love of the ages and nothing could shatter that. Ruth and Harold were the star-crossed lovers of legends.

A compassionate warden allowed the two a few moments together after the last stay of execution had been denied by the governor, and Harold and Ruth pledged their eternal fidelity that would endure beyond the tomb.

"Ruth was scheduled to go first," my father told me. "And when we saw her, it was a sight to break your heart. Her beauty shone through the rough prison clothes and the ugliness of the scene was banished by a sort of saintliness that seemed to radiate from her like a halo. I even found myself doubting her guilt as they brought her into the room, toward that terrible chair with its heavy leather straps. She looked around and her eyes met mine and when she spoke, it was as if she were reaching down into my heart. 'Love will endure,' she said. 'Remember that. We were fools, but we loved.' Then, as they led her toward the chair, her face changed, and it was all the matrons could do to hold her. She looked at me again and her voice was a horrid shriek as she pleaded, 'No! Take Harold first! Take *him!*' Ben, me lad, I hope you never have to listen

157

to a human creature debasing itself as that poor woman did, calling for us to kill her lover first, so that she might have another ten precious minutes of the scrap of life."

Now it was my time to plead. And if I thought it would have done any good, I *would* have pleaded. But there was no help to be had through mercy. Jesse and Hodge were not men to be moved by pity. I was dangerous to them, so it's over the side, Ben old boy, no hard feelings.

"Right here," said Hodge. The engine slowed.

"Give me a boost," said Jesse.

Rough hands grabbed me and lifted me up onto the transom.

Jesse's eyes met mine. He smiled. "Here's your chance, Ben," he said. "Go investigate your sharks."

In the tough detective fiction movies that was my cue to spit in his eye. But in life, I was hyperventilating my lungs, trying to buy that extra fifteen or twenty seconds of underwater life that might mean all the difference between oblivion and survival.

"Roll him over," said Hodge.

They did.

16

THE TOP of the water was warm, but as I sank, it grew chilly. If my hands had merely been tied behind my back, I might have been able to tread water and even swim, after a fashion. But bound as I was, even if my water-logged clothes would have permitted me to float, my head was drawn back in such a way that it would have been underneath the surface.

I heard a dull throb in the water as the boat sped away.

Each time I moved my hands, the rope bit into my neck and choked me. Once I gasped and sucked in salt water, and it took all my will power to keep from exhaling and losing what oxygen I had remaining.

I got my fingers around the Philippine fighting knife and managed to draw it out of my sock. Getting it open was harder, fraught with the danger of dropping it from my numb fingers and losing all hope of escape. But I managed to separate the split wooden handle and, unseen, the blade emerged. I pressed it against the rope around my ankles and began to saw back and forth.

Braided nylon anchor rope is hard to cut under the best

159

of circumstances. These were not such circumstances. Blinded by the salt water, my chest burning from lack of air, my movements hampered by the constricting bonds, I worked frantically and it was almost as much luck as skill that finally parted the rope.

Able to straighten up in the water, I kicked my way to the surface. As I did, the knife slipped from my hand and sank toward the bottom of the Gulf.

Light flooded my eyes as I burst into the air. With the pressure from my ankles slackened, I was able to slip my hands from the loops of rope, and now it was fastened only to my neck.

Hungrily, I gulped down deep breaths of air. They were flavored with salt spray. Quickly, I looked around to see where the Chris Craft was. If they saw me, it would be easy to double back and run me down.

But it was already out of sight, at least from my point of view only a few inches above the churning waves.

I held my breath, ducked under the water, and pulled off my shoes. The sports jacket went next. I was debating the wisdom of taking off my trousers and tying the legs to try to fill them with air to make a life preserver when I heard the steady pealing of a bell.

As a long swell lifted me higher, I saw a red channel buoy a hundred feet away. It was rocking back and forth in the waves.

I swam to it. It wasn't big enough to climb up on, but it floated and gave me something to hang on to.

160

How far was shore? I searched for it. Too far to swim, until I was rested at least.

Well, I was safe enough here. At least, unless one of those requiem sharks located me.

That was not a pleasant thought. It seemed unlikely that a convenient killer shark would be waiting around whenever the Cabin One boys wanted to heave somebody in the drink. But then, how had it been possible for a school of them to be waiting when Guy Pritchard fell overboard, eighteen miles out to sea?

The buoy bell clanged in my ear. Beethoven never wrote sweeter music.

Then I heard another sound. This one was unwelcome.

The steady throb of an engine.

It sounded as if Jesse and Hodge were coming back. I looked around for the boat, but I couldn't see it. The sound grew louder.

I found the cable that held the buoy anchored to the sea bed and, holding my breath, clutched it and pulled myself under the water. The engine noise was louder there. I stayed down as long as I could.

The engine came closer. It throttled down. Someone was waiting up there. I held my breath as long as I could, then pulled myself gently up the cable, hoping the buoy would be between me and the boat.

It wasn't. I surfaced almost directly in front of its prow.

But it wasn't the Chris Craft. It was Fred Bellavia's beat-up bait boat.

161

He threw a rope ladder over the side. I hauled myself, dripping, up it and fell down in the scuppers. Bellavia rummaged around in the cockpit and handed me a bottle. I drank from it and nearly strangled. It was straight corn whiskey.

"I thought I saw some commotion near here," he said. "So I waited until that other boat left and scooted over."

"I'm glad you did," I gasped. "I don't think I could have hacked the swim to shore."

"Good thing you didn't try," he said. "There's a real rip tide off the point here. You sure are one for trouble, aren't you? First paying seventy-five cents for a beer, and now getting yourself throwed overboard. Mr. Shock, you need a keeper."

"I need a ship-to-shore radio," I said. "And I bet you haven't got one."

"That's the first time you won," he said. "Don't need one on this old scow. I've got one on my own boat, though."

"Which is?"

"Little old forty-six-foot Dolphin," he said blandly.

"Well, in case you didn't recognize them, the boys who threw me overboard were your buddies from Cabin One."

"I was afraid you might get in trouble on account of me letting you near that key. Now you done lost your shoes and your coat, and I lost me four good paying customers."

"Maybe we can get Chief Gautier to take over their room and board, if we get in soon enough."

"Not unless they're duck stupid," he said. "They'll be

long gone by the time we dock."

And, of course, they were. The Chris Craft was still there, but it had been scuttled and was bow-deep in the water.

"That's just plain mean," complained Bellavia. "We won't have any trouble raising her to get the engine numbers in case the registration's phony."

"But it'll take time," I said, "and that's what they're buying."

They'd bought more, too, by letting the air out of the Fleetwood's tires. The scratches on its hood showed they'd tried to get inside to take off the distributor cap, but the double lock I'd installed keeps intruders out unless they know where the secret catch is.

I used Bellavia's phone to call the Triple A, whom I have found a godsend on numerous back stretches of our country's highways, and told them my problem. They promised to send a tow truck and an extra wheel so they could replace one of the flats, the other one to be replaced with my spare, and then they would tow the Fleetwood in to be fixed up.

I pleaded for a 7 P.M. completion and they assured it. Then I called The Old Place and asked for Charity. Lisa Dantzler answered.

"She's not here, Mr. Shock."

"Well, will you give her a message?"

"Perhaps."

Nice lady. But then, Ben, she's been through a lot. Be nice. "Tell her I had a little car trouble, but I'll be out that way as soon as I can get a cab."

"Very well." There was a pause. "Dr. Marconi is here. She'd like to speak with you."

"Put her on."

Another pause. Then: "Ben?"

"That's me."

"Where are you?"

"Bellavia's Fishing Camp."

"I've got a taxi here," she said. "Wait there. I want to talk with you."

"I've *got* to wait here," I said. "My car's got four flats."

She said, "Four?"

"And I don't have any shoes. Before you leave, would you look in my room and get the extra pair in the closet? Oh, and my plaid jacket?"

"Ben! Did you lose your clothes?"

"Be a nice shark doctor and do like I say."

"All right," she said. "But don't blame me for what Lisa may think."

As I hung up and went over to get some of the hot tea Fred Bellavia was brewing, it occurred to me that it did not now, and never *had,* interest me what Lisa Dantzler thought.

Next time, I decided, *I* am going to pick the clients. Charity's automatic telephone has had a lousy average.

"I checked out Number One," Bellavia said. "They've flown the coop. If you want, I'll get together the information I have on them. Chances are it's all phony."

"Better do it anyway. I'll check in with Gautier."

164

"Have some tea first. Number One's unlocked. You can go over there and freshen up. There's towels and if you put the air conditioner on Heat instead of Cool, it'll dry your clothes in just a couple of minutes."

"The garage is coming to pick up my car."

"I'll take care of it."

I thanked him and padded my barefooted way over to the cabin in which I'd been surprised just a short hour ago. I was, all things considered, very lucky to be doing it.

I rinsed the salt out of my double-knit slacks and hung them up in front of the air conditioner. Now was their moment of truth. We would see how good those miracle garments really were. I did the same for my shirt and shorts and crawled under a warm shower to wash off the salt water and the smell of fear.

There was a tap at the door. "Come on in," I said.

Someone did. I turned off the water and stepped out of the shower, reaching for a towel. "Did they come for the car, Fred?"

Jerri Marconi said, "I wouldn't know."

17

THERE'S NO POINT in describing it all, is there? These days all the words have been used, and down on 42nd Street you can buy books with all the pictures, too. It was something neither of us consciously intended, but it happened and it sprang naturally out of the momentary embarrassment I had about standing there in my birthday suit, and from Jerri's teasing and from some unspoken attraction we had somehow formed for each other in just a few hours. It wasn't what we know as Love, but it wasn't just empty fulfillment either. And I was glad it had happened.

I sat up suddenly, remembering James Copeland and his geriatic Nash. "My God! Jimmy's meter is running and so will his mouth."

"Too late, my hero," Jerri said, pulling me back down onto the too-narrow bed. "I've been in here too long to save anything from the situation. Three minutes with the door closed and it's all over town."

"You don't sound very penitent," I said.

166

"I'm not. I was curious, and now my curiosity has been satisfied."

"For the better, I hope."

She traced the line of my jaw. "Very much for the better, dear Ben. I was not disappointed in a single anticipation of my lurid imagination. You are a very sweet, a very gentle man. They should have named you Ferdinand."

"I never liked flowers."

"And a very sad man, too."

"I live in interesting times."

She kissed my chest. "You must love her very much."

What the hell was the point in trying to lie? This was no stupid in bed with me. "I do," I said. "But it's a long story."

"Which you do not intend to tell me."

"It wouldn't help."

"I suppose not," she said. "It never helps anyone except the teller, and I imagine you're strong enough to shoulder your troubles by yourself."

"You ought to hear me whimper when I get up in the morning."

"I'd like that." She kissed me again. "But I won't."

"No," I said. "I guess you won't."

She got up suddenly and slapped my stomach. "Me for a shower," she said. "Watch that Jax, Ferdinand. It can lump up on you."

"You're telling me," I said. I suppose I should have

showered again, too, but I was in a hurry, so I pulled on my now-dry clothes and slipped on the loafers she'd brought. She came out of the tiny shower stall all ruddy and glowing from the heat. I sat there sipping at one of the cans of Jax my buddies had left and watched her with a quiet pleasure, and wished that it could be something more.

She dropped me at the garage where they were already nearly finished reviving my Fleetwood. I took her into a coffee shop and we each had a cup of brown poison.

"It got lost somewhere in the confusion," I said. "You wanted to talk to me."

Flustered, she stammered, "Oh, yes, I mean—"

"Sip your coffee," I said. "It will restore the dead. This brew could be used in NASA's second-stage engines."

She choked on it. "You're right."

"Now, speak."

"When I was talking with the lab, I had a thought. My superintendent—"

"Your janitor."

"Anyway, he checked for me. There's a gallon container of shark scent missing, Ben."

"The stuff that attracts them?"

"Yes."

"How far would a gallon go?"

"If you used it sensibly, you could probably call every shark in the Gulf."

"Be specific."

"Well," she said thoughtfully, "if you made a drag

168

track, like I described, there'd be forty or fifty applications at least."

"For how great a distance?"

"Until it dispersed in the water. I'd say each application would treat a five- or six-mile trail in the absence of any strong underwater currents."

That explained a lot. "How about your janitor? Can you trust him?"

"He's almost seventy years old and he goes to revival meeting every other night."

"Who else can get into the lab?"

"When it's locked up? Nobody. But it isn't locked often —as you found out today. Anybody could walk in and take what he wanted."

"But he'd have to know what it was he wanted."

"Yes," she said. "I suppose he would."

We finished the coffee. It was the only decent thing to do. Had we left it, the waitress might have poured it down the sink and polluted the sewage system. I paid and we went outside.

"What now?" Jerri asked.

"Now I go out to The Old Place and try to fit a few pieces of the puzzle together."

"With Charity?"

"Yes."

"What about us?"

I squeezed her hand. "What *about* us?"

"Is this it?"

Quite a question from quite a girl. It was tempting. Who

169

would it harm? We were both consenting adults. We weren't lying to each other or even to ourselves. It was as good a way as any to spend a hurricane.

What had happened had been more than pleasurable. It had been spontaneous and honest and rewarding.

But now? In cold blood? The name would change. *It* would change. And although I have never been rated Outstanding in Character, there are some things that just don't work for me.

"I guess it is, baby," I said.

She nodded. "I knew it."

She bent forward and kissed me. Her eyelashes fluttered against my cheek. They were damp. What the hell, maybe mine were, too. Then she got in the cab and drove away. I felt like someone standing on a train platform in a Noel Coward play.

The Fleetwood was ready. I signed the AAA slip for the tow, paid for the rest of the work, and was on my way.

Another day, another lay.

Ah, Ben, you gay dog! Was it you who said all those hard-hitting suspense stories were so much fodder for wet dreams? Look at you, sweeping lovely young scientists off their feminine feet on a moment's acquaintance. Move over, Mike Hammer! Ben Shock is in town.

So why did I feel even sadder and meaner as I drove west on Route 90? Hell, I'd scored, hadn't I?

Sure. Good guys: everything. Ben Shock: zero.

The new grave in the cemetery was ready for its occupant. The tent was up, the chairs were in place. And the wind nibbled persistently at it all.

There were two strange cars outside The Old Place. I parked my Fleetwood behind the last one and went in through the back way that we hired hands always use.

Margaret was in the kitchen making sandwiches.

"Mr. Shock," she said. "Miss Tucker's been looking for you."

"Where is she?"

"In the library."

I followed her indicating finger and went into a dark, book-lined room. Charity was curled up on the couch in front of an electric fireplace that looked warmer than the actual thing. But it just flickered without heat.

She leaped up. "Ben! Lisa told me that—Marconi—went out of here with a change of clothes for you. What happened? Are you all right?"

"Drip-Dry Shock, that's me," I said, helping myself to a drink from the decanter on a tray. "It seems there's four bully-boys who have been basing themselves down at Bellavia's Fishing Camp, heading out every now and then in a fast boat pretending to be fishermen. My guess is they've been going out to the tower and causing a little trouble."

"But—" Her hand indicated my baggy trousers which, despite the advertising claims, had *not* restored themselves to pristine beauty after getting wet.

"They caught me and decided I should go for a little swim a mile out."

171

What was I supposed to do, describe the fear and the terrible nearness of death? You play it light because you have to.

"Where does your blonde friend fit in?"

"You weren't here. I had to throw off my shoes and coat to keep from going to the bottom. She delivered new ones."

"Some delivery lady," Charity said. I could tell she'd been very worried about me. But now that I was safe, it was spanking time. "I suppose you asked her to deliver some perfume, too."

"Baby—"

"Don't baby me, you bastard!" she said. "Since when do you wear Chanel Number Five?"

"So I gave her a hug—"

"Liar. We both know what you gave her. You don't come home reeking like a perfume counter from just hugging."

I couldn't protest too vigorously. After all, she was right. I reached for her. "Charity, listen to me—"

Fast as a cat's paw flicking, she threw the remainder of her drink in my face. I didn't have time to blink. The Scotch burned my eyes and ran down my cheeks.

"Don't touch me, Ben," she said softly. "Don't even come near me. You stink of her."

Mad, I said, "Maybe yes, maybe no. But you're doing your best to make sure I do, assuming I don't already."

"Get out of here."

"Gladly. How far out? Is my bedroom far enough? Or

shall I just get in the car and go back to New York?"

She turned away. "I don't care where you go."

Translation: I want you to stay, but I won't ask.

I said, "That's clear enough. It won't take me long to pack."

Translation: I want to stay too, but unless you stop me, I'm going.

I turned and left the room.

18

THE FIRST RULE about skirmishes on the Field of Eros is that they must always be taken seriously. No matter how aware you may be of the rigid mating-dance sequence, there is no way you can throw up your hands and laugh and say, "What the hell are we going through all this for?" and leap ahead to the desired result. Each volley must be fired and its casualties must be taken. Only when both antagonists are drained and spent can there be serious peace negotiations.

Sometimes I feel that the behavior of national governments is closer to the acts of jealous lovers than to any rational interchange of ideas. And vice versa.

I packed my suitcase. It took a fast three minutes. Who the hell did Charity Tucker think she was anyway? We weren't married. We weren't even vowed. Nobody tells Ben Shock what to do. There are no strings on me. Isn't that the way the litany goes?

So I got undressed and took a shower. A long one. That gave her another ten minutes.

It was enough. When I came out, wrapped in a towel

(I had learned my lesson about bursting naked from showers like Venus from the Sea), she was waiting.

"I see you didn't waste any time packing."

"No."

Translation: You should have been up here five minutes ago.

"So you're going to run out on the case. I thought you were a professional."

Translation: Stay.

"You ought to run out on it, too. This is a sticky one. It can get dangerous."

Translation: Let's *both* of us blow this town.

"I know," she said. "What I found out this afternoon—" She looked down at her hands curled in her lap. "Ben, I'm sorry. Don't go."

That didn't need any translation.

One of us had to reach out and touch the other. She had come as far as she could go. So I went the rest of the way.

She clutched me, weeping against my shoulder.

"Oh, Ben," she said. "It's my fault. I can't blame you. How wretchedly frustrated you must be all the time. I'm sorry. It isn't your problem. You *ought* to go. I'm bad news."

"Hush," I said.

"But I want you to understand—"

"I said hush, or I'll stuff a pillow in your mouth."

"You wouldn't dare."

"Try me."

She giggled. "You would, wouldn't you?"

I tugged at the towel which was trying to work its way down to the rug. "Let's talk business. What did you find out that upset you so much?"

"Maybe you were right about our Miss Lisa. Do you know what she and brother-in-law Nick Wiggins did this morning while we were out on that Texas Tower?"

"Tell me."

"There's a little town upstate called Harlon. They drove up there and took out a marriage license."

The towel gave up and deserted. I padded over and slipped into a pair of shorts. "You have to be kidding."

"I wish I were. Did you ever hear of such bad taste?"

"The hell with taste. That provides the one thing we've been missing all along. Motive. But you'd think they would have better sense than to make it so obvious."

"You said this was a bad one. It may be so bad that we won't get paid. If we send Lisa up as an accomplice to murder, she isn't going to be exactly delighted to write us a nice check."

I frowned. "But why sabotage her own oil operation? That's the goose that lays the eggs."

"To divert suspicion elsewhere?"

"Maybe. Or maybe the two aren't even connected. On the one hand, organized mischief. On the other, the old familiar crime of passion."

"And sharks mixed up in both? I find that a little hard to take."

"Me, too." I opened the suitcase and took out the J. T. S. Brown. "I don't know what good manners are when you may be getting ready to bust your boss for murder. But I don't think Ann Landers would want us to drink Miss Lisa's liquor."

I mixed us two weak ones with tap water from the sink.

"Who knows about this license?" I asked.

"Nobody," she said. "Not in town, that is. My guy from WWL had asked his station research people to keep an eye on anything involving the Dantzlers. It popped up on the vital statistics teletype late this afternoon. He called me from New Orleans, and I asked him not to mention it around here in case there might be a mistake. After all, Lisa and Nick have both been through a lot and if we're wrong, it would be crummy to add to their troubles."

"Good girl. But something tells me you've hit it."

"What do we do?"

"Brace him with it. And make sure that my trusty .38 is within reaching distance. Although I don't believe that either of them is the type to go in for personal violence. They hire someone else to do the dirty work."

"Maybe you ought to call Chief Gautier."

"That's not our job," I said. "Our job was to help Lisa combat the harassment she's been having over the oil operation. And, later, to check into Millie's death. At this moment, neither shark killing has been called murder by anyone. Gautier's investigating. So are we. If our digging comes up with murder, we'll have to turn it over to him. But if it doesn't—if there's only a little case of hanky-pank between Lisa and her sister's husband—our assignment is to keep the law as far away as possible."

"You make us sound like the hired guns the good citizens of Dodge City used to bring in to throw out the bad guys."

"So?"

She sighed. "So I'll go downstairs and make nice talk with Nick. He's half in the bag already. You know that they're planning the funeral for eight A.M. tomorrow?"

"If Hilda doesn't interfere."

"The latest weather report has her stationary between Cuba and the Mexican coast."

"Okay, try to keep him sober. I'll get dressed and be right down."

She turned at the door. "Ben?"

"What?"

"Don't forget your pistol."

"I won't. Have you got your handy-dandy cassette recorder ready to go?"

"It's in my purse. It'll be near enough to pick up everything he says."

"Good."

She left, and I got myself together again. My head ached. I don't know why. It should have gotten used to being banged around by now.

I went downstairs. Nick was, as Charity had put it, half in the bag. He had a dark drink in his hand.

"Come on," he urged. "It's the Happy Hour."

"I want to talk to you, Nick."

"Not without a drink."

178

I made my own. He would have poured me one of the bombs he was having.

Charity had gone out into the living room when I arrived, but I saw that her purse was near Nick on a table. Inside, I knew, was a tiny Nagra recorder, voice actuated. It only worked when somebody was talking, and shut off in between. Saves batteries and tape.

Nick Wiggins lifted his glass in a mock toast.

"To happiness."

"I'll drink to that." I did. "Nick, I hate to brace you with this just now, but it's important."

"You found out," he said, with the confidential nod of the half-drunk. "I told her it was stupid, but she insisted."

"Who insisted on what?"

He dug into his pocket and came out with a crumpled handful of torn paper. He scattered it onto a coffee table like confetti.

"Lisa insisted on this. She was distraught. I went along because I wanted to help." He stirred the pile of paper. "If you put this jigsaw together, you'll find it's a marriage license issued today to Miss Lisa Dantzler and Mr. Nicholas Conrad Wiggins, widower." He worked on his drink. "An all-around lousy idea, and as you can see, one I never intended to go through with."

"Whether you did or not isn't my business. But why the hurry?"

He fixed one bleary eye on me. "You're nobody's fool, Ben. You must know about the old bastard's trust arrangement on Dantzler Oil."

"A little."

"Pima Indians, for Christ's sake! That cracker would rather expiate an old guilt than protect his own daughters. Not that it surprised me. He always wanted sons, hated the girls for their sex, tormented them with their inadequacy. What the hell do you think turned Lisa into such a ballbuster? The Right Honorable Amos Dantzler, lawyer, retired judge, oil magnate and thief of both Indian and women's rights." He lifted his glass again. "Let's drink to the bastard!"

"Okay, he made a lousy deal for Lisa and Millie. What's that got to do with your torn-up marriage license?"

"These southern states have some peculiar laws," he said. "Particularly Louisiana, which recognizes one referred to as the Napoleonic Code, which, to simplify, is a form of community property except that the spouse doesn't have to wait until death or divorce to collect his or her share. I've been working on a scheme to break that oil trust based on my rights under the Napoleonic Code."

"I thought Millie's will and the terms of the trust both rule out any inheritance to the husband."

"They do. But such rulings might be overturned as not being in the public interest. Frankly, I think the government of these two states would rather see control of Dantzler Oil remain in the hands of the Dantzlers or even the Wigginses rather than be turned over to the Pima Indians."

Well, why not? We've been screwing the Indians ever

180

since Columbus landed on San Salvador and put them to fetching water for his crew.

"That still doesn't explain this hurry to marry Millie's sister."

He laughed. "I never intended to marry her, Ben. She's frantic that what's going on will strike her next, and her assumption is that there's safety in numbers. If there're two of us to put out of the way, they may not be so quick to move."

"That's assuming, of course, that someone actually *is* trying to put the Dantzlers out of the way."

"Well, isn't that a reasonable assumption in view of what's happened?"

"It's a possible one. But there are also other possibilities." I looked at the heap of torn paper. "So you just went along with Lisa's plan to keep her from being nervous."

"That's right. If it would make her feel better, why not? It'll take a few days to get a reading on whether or not my attempts to break the trust on the grounds of my marriage to Millie will still be viable. If they are, there isn't any reason for me to marry Lisa."

"Don't you like the lady?"

"Sure I like her. But not to marry."

"So it's the money you're after."

"Yes. But not for myself. Originally, I wanted to preserve it for Lisa and Millie. Now only Lisa's left, but the plan's the same."

I studied him. It was a big one to swallow, but Robin Hoods *have* existed. Besides, as it now stood, he had no

181

reason to want either of the sisters dead; quite the opposite
—Millie's killing had only made his case tougher.

"Okay," I said. "But when you tell Lisa you've torn up
that license, I advise you to duck."

"I'm not telling her," he said. "Not until I know where
we stand vis-à-vis the trust. Why increase her tension?"

"You tell me," I said, finishing my drink.

The wind gusted against the windows. Nick Wiggins
stared at them. Rain was beginning to pattern the glass
with tiny droplets.

"She's in no danger," he said finally. "She just thinks
she is. If I thought there was a chance—" He stopped.
"I'm drunk," he said. "Don't pay any attention to me."

Charity came in. "Nick," she said, "sorry to bother you,
but there's a Reverend Fowlkes here to see you."

Nick nodded sadly. "Yes," he said. "We have to get our
heads together and decide on what lies to tell during the
sermon."

He left the room unsteadily. Charity opened her purse
and switched off the recorder.

"Get anything, Ben?"

"Only that everybody's out to screw the Pima Indians.
But as far as I can see, Nick doesn't have the slightest
reason in the world to want to hamper Dantzler drilling
operations. If they lose money, *he* loses money."

"What about those four men down at the fishing
camp?"

"Gautier's trying to check them out. But somebody had

182

to have hired them. The question is, who's got anything to gain?"

"Us," she said. "If we solve the case, we get paid. Maybe we're the guilty ones."

"In that case," I said, "turn us in so I can get some rest."

"You don't look well," she said, concerned. "Maybe that wasn't a joke. Maybe you ought to go to bed."

"I'm going to the nearest restaurant where I can get a thick steak and two martinis straight up and a bottle of red wine."

"You'll hate yourself in the morning," she told me.

"My head couldn't feel any worse than it does right now. Are you coming with me?"

"Is that for real, or is it just a 'Y'all come see us, y'hear?' Have you noticed, Ben, that in the south the word is equal to the deed? If you invite someone to visit, hoping they won't come, and they *don't,* you're still one up, because in your own mind, having invited, you've extended the hospitality that wasn't actually ever received."

"Bitter, bitter," I said.

"No," she smiled. "Just observant."

"Well, it's a real invitation."

"You don't have your blonde stashed down in some motel?"

"If I did, I wouldn't tell. Gentlemen never do."

"Ha!" she said.

We found a nice restaurant over near Gulfport, and

while the steak wasn't aged, it was tender and flavorful. The martinis were too full of vermouth, but I drank them anyway, and the wine was California and chilled, and we drank that, too, and drove home slightly squiffed.

I kissed Charity good night at her bedroom door, went to mine, undressed and crawled between the sheets.

My head felt much better.

I waited for what seemed a very long time before I drifted into sleep, and she did not come.

19

IT WAS a good day for a funeral—dark, humid, a lowering gray sky that sat atop the wind-bent pines with an oppressive gloom.

A tap at the door awakened me.

"Okay," I said. "I'm awake."

"Wear your dark suit," said Charity's voice.

Sure. I always carry it, because unlike the private eyes I've read about or seen in the movies, somehow I get to attend all the funerals. Hell, in those movies, I don't think they even *bury* the victims. You see them fall down, and then they're forgotten. Maybe the streetcleaner picks them up.

I shaved and dressed and went downstairs.

This time, my .38 was snugged down inside my coat. It made a slight lump, but I didn't figure anybody was going to be frisking funeral guests. And if I was going to be a private cop, it was time I started dressing like one. Maybe I would get myself a black shirt and a yellow necktie, too.

There was a kind of buffet brunch laid out in the dining room. Nobody was paying it much attention. Charity was drinking coffee, and so was Nick Wiggins, except I bet myself silently that his was half brandy. His eyes looked like two powder-burned bullet holes in his head. His hands shook and the coffee slopped over into the saucer.

Lisa Dantzler was in a furious argument with Uncle Edgar Dantzler.

"You're a selfish old man!" she said.

"Just leave me be, Lisa," he said. He was wearing faded blue pants and a tattered green shirt. Hardly proper for a funeral.

"Let him alone, Lisa," said Nick. "If he doesn't want to go to the funeral, leave him here."

"You stay out of this," she shot back with a venom that hardly fitted one who was, presumably, trying to lead Nick to the altar.

"Yes, ma'am," Nick said, turning away.

In an undertone, Charity said to me, "I don't give their marriage a year."

"Shh."

"I don't have to go to the graveyard to see the burying," said Uncle Edgar. "I got my telescope up in the light-house. I see good from there." He looked around the room —at Nick, at Lisa, then at Grover Ellis, who had just been ushered in by Margaret. "I see everything. So don't tell me where to go and what to do. I see more than you give me credit for."

He stormed out of the room.

"The car's ready," said Ellis.

"Let's go," said Lisa, glaring at Nick.

186

He finished his coffee. She took his arm and they left, followed by Ellis.

"It sounds more like they're late for a football game than a funeral," I said.

"What do you think Uncle Edgar meant?" Charity asked.

"I think he was trying to get under someone's skin. And he may have succeeded. Has Ross Gautier been around this morning?"

"Earlier. He left, but he said he'll be at the funeral."

I swallowed half a cup of Margaret's coffee. It hadn't improved overnight. "I'm with Uncle Edgar," I said. "I don't want to go to this bash either."

"It won't take long."

"Okay," I said. "But only because I want to talk with Gautier."

The wind was really gusting now. As I started the Fleetwood, I asked, "What's the hurricane news?"

"Bad. It's heading right for us."

"Then why didn't they postpone the funeral? The way it's blowing, we may all need one."

"Ask Lisa."

"I may just do that." I drove up the narrow road and parked outside the church. There were several other cars there. Hardly a full-house turnout.

"There's the Chief, over by the gravesite," said Charity.

"You stay in the car," I said. "It's getting wet out there."

I went over and cornered Gautier.

"You and me are out of business, officially," he said. "The coroner's jury came in with verdicts of accidental death for both Millie Wiggins and Guy Pritchard."

"Well, I think there's someone you ought to question before you close the files."

"Who's that?"

"Lisa's Uncle Edgar. He dropped a pretty broad hint this morning that he'd seen something out of that lighthouse perch of his besides the passing sea gulls."

The wind tumbled a small tree branch past us. Gautier looked around. "They better hurry, or it's going to be too late."

"How bad can it get?"

"Bad enough. As it stands, she's aimed right at us. But they usually turn off when they near the land."

"If she doesn't?"

"She'd better. We've gotten a little too careless the past ten years. A few broken windows, some water damage— what the hell, we figure, those hurricanes aren't that bad. But if we ever get hit solid, it'll be a different story. If there's the right combination of wind and tide, this whole coastline could be swept away."

"Great. Why do people live here?"

"Why do people live right on top of the San Andreas fault in San Francisco? We're betting it doesn't happen. So far it hasn't. Knock wood."

The church bell began to chime. People came out, bending their heads into the wind.

188

Charity came over and joined us. Then Nick and Lisa and Ellis arrived, with Margaret and several men I recognized from the oil rig. It looked as if Ellis had closed it down as he said he might.

The pallbearers brought the coffin to the grave and lowered it onto the supports there. It was made of gleaming silver-colored metal.

I heard someone sobbing near me. I looked. It was Jerri Marconi. Ross Gautier patted her shoulder.

Reverend Fowlkes was reading something from his prayer book. He had difficulty. The wind ripped the pages and tried to tear the book from his hands. Rain drove against our faces like tiny needles. Finally, he finished, and the funeral group moved away from the grave.

I caught Gautier's eye and jerked my thumb toward the lighthouse, towering over the pine trees. He nodded.

Charity and I got back in the Fleetwood and drove to The Old Place.

"I'll be right in," I said. "I want to get Uncle Edgar. The Chief's got a few questions for him."

"I figured that was what you were up to," she said.

I stuck my head inside the lighthouse door and yelled, "Uncle Edgar?"

My voice echoed up the winding stairway like Mantovani, but there wasn't any answer.

I yelled again, and then I went up and found him.

He was slumped over his old-fashioned brass telescope

with one of his own bayonets impaling him between the shoulders.

Whoever had done it had been in a hurry. They'd left before the old man was dead. And, in a finger dipped with his own blood, he had written a name, and now everything fell into place for me.

20

THE HOUSE was full of people.

I barely made it. The wind was howling fiercely and small objects were being hurtled through the air like missiles.

The people were gathered in front of the TV set, where a weatherman from New Orleans was urging all beach residents to barricade themselves in the center of their homes, away from windows.

"If you haven't already evacuated," he warned, "don't try now. It's too late. You're safer in your homes than you would be in the open."

"We're trapped," Charity said cheerfully as I came in.

"What happened to the U.S. Weather Service?" I asked. "I thought they were supposed to let us know in time."

"Somebody fouled up," Gautier said sourly. "Hilda suddenly started moving and picked up wind velocity before they knew what was happening."

Lisa said, "The library's the safest room. Everybody, get in there."

"Where are you going?" I asked.

"To open windows on opposite sides of the house," she said. "It equalizes the pressure. The rugs may get wet, but at least the roof shouldn't blow off."

"I'll help," I said.

As I left, I gave Charity a wink.

"We'll be all right, won't we?" I asked, simulating nervousness as I helped Lisa open windows on the shore side of the house. "I mean, this place must have been through dozens of these storms."

"Don't worry, Mr. Shock," she said. "I haven't lost a private investigator yet. That is, if you *are* an investigator. So far I haven't seen much in the way of results."

"That might be due to your own busy schedule," I said. "It's pretty complicated, preparing for both a funeral and a marriage."

"Marriage?" She turned and ran her fingers through her wind-tousled blonde hair. "What do you mean?"

"I mean the license you and Nick took out yesterday."

"Mr. Shock," she said, "if this is a joke, it's in very bad taste."

"It's not a joke," I told her. "I saw it myself."

"Well, of all the outrageous—"

If she was faking, she had wasted her time in the oil business. She could have won an Oscar on the screen.

That was the last nagging question I'd had to ask. Now I was ready.

We went back into the library. Just as we did, the lights flickered and went out.

"Power's gone," Gautier said unnecessarily.

"There's a battery-operated radio by the fireplace," Lisa said. Grover Ellis turned it on. Static rasped, then a voice told us that we weren't to become panic-stricken, but to get the hell off the roads *right now,* because winds were gusting up to seventy miles an hour and it looked like Hilda was headed straight for Gulfport.

I caught Gautier's eye while the others were listening intently to the radio and muttered into his ear. He nodded.

Margaret came in carrying a huge tray of sandwiches. "I used up everything in the icebox," she said. She put it down and started to go back to the kitchen.

"Stay here," I said. "It's safer."

She gave me a surprised look, but sat down. Lisa Dantzler opened her mouth, then closed it again.

The last time I'd seen a gathering like this was in one of those Thin Man detective movies. All the suspects gathered in one place, trapped there by a storm, or the reading of a will, or perhaps a native uprising outside.

"There's bad news," I said. "Lisa, your Uncle Edgar is dead. Murdered. This time there's no doubt."

"Stop it!" she said shrilly.

"I'm sorry," I said. "Chief, he's in the lightroom of the lighthouse. He managed to leave a message before he died. I think you ought to go up and look at it, in case the storm destroys the evidence. Take Charity with you as a witness."

"Right," he said. Then he glared around and said the obligatory line: "Nobody leaves this room."

He and Charity went out the back way. It was easy to

193

tell when they opened the door. The air pressure rose sharply and a whining howl of wind overwhelmed the radio voice. Papers scattered and Jerri Marconi screamed.

Nick Wiggins held her hand and she quieted down. Lisa stared at them. I met her eye and gave a little shake of my head. I didn't want her giving away my secret until I was ready.

"Why would anyone want to kill poor Uncle Edgar?" she said. "He wasn't very likable, but he was harmless."

"He was also a nosy old man," I said, "and that was anything *but* harmless to those who found out that he'd been watching them secretly from his perch in the lighthouse."

"What could he have seen?" Nick said. "Oh, we've had some wild parties here, I'll admit that. But—"

"If Uncle Edgar was anything like most old men I've known," I said, "he probably roamed around at all hours of the night and early morning. Maybe he saw some private parties you didn't know about. Maybe he even saw what happened the night Millie was killed."

"Well," he said, "*you* saw that."

"Not exactly. I saw Millie come out of the house. At least I thought she came out of the house. As we all know, she was nude, and she jumped into the pool without realizing there was a shark there."

"We've been through all that." This was Lisa, who still didn't trust me or believe what I'd told her while we were closing windows.

"Well, *why* didn't she know there was a shark there?

Not that she'd expect to find one, but the pool was lighted, and a ten-foot shark isn't exactly something that hides under a lily pad."

"You tell us," said Nick.

"She was in the garage with someone. Since she was nude, we can imagine what they were doing. And she probably had a little drink or two. A couple of drops of any of a dozen drugs you can buy from the local head shop will make a person so bleary-eyed she couldn't spot an elephant if it stood on her toe. But when Millie emerged, she ran right into two strangers. Charity and yours truly. She didn't know who we were, probably couldn't even see our faces. So she did just what the murderer wanted her to do—she jumped into the pool anyway—but to hide her nakedness from us, not to go skinny-dipping with her boy friend."

"Those are terrible accusations, Ben," said Lisa. "Millie wasn't like that."

"You mean she wouldn't play around?" I stared at her. "Are you so sure?"

She lowered her eyes.

The back door opened and the wind howled through the room again. Gautier and Charity staggered in. They were drenched.

"You were right, Ben," he said. "The old man wrote a name before he died." He turned to Grover Ellis. "Ellis, it's my duty to advise you—"

Ellis hauled out his .44 Ruger Blackhawk.

"Knock it off, Grover," said Gautier, reaching for his

own weapon. "I know you always carry that thing empty." Ellis squeezed the trigger and a bullet plowed into the floor between the Chief's feet.

"Easy now," said the oilman. "Toss your gun over here. Use just two fingers."

"I can't get it out of the holster that way," Gautier grumbled. "Miss Dantzler, you take it!"

Lisa did, holding it away from her body. She dropped it at Grover's feet.

"Now, Shock. Yours, too."

I slipped it out and let it slide to the floor. Lisa picked it up and put it near Gautier's.

Numbly, Nick Wiggins said, "Whose name was written up there?"

"What do you think?" said Gautier. "The old man wrote 'Ellis' in his own blood."

"I didn't do it," Ellis said. "But if you think I'm going to hang around here and get myself railroaded by a bunch of red-necked hicks—"

Quietly, Nick said, "You won't be railroaded, Grover. Think. The coroner's jury decided that the two shark deaths were accidental. And whoever killed the old man must have had both a reason and an opportunity. You had neither. You were up at the funeral with us when it happened."

Ellis hesitated. "They'll twist it around. They'll pin it on me somehow. You—"

Nick's hand had been in his jacket pocket as he sat on

196

the couch. Now flame erupted through the tweed and as the sound of a shot blasted through the room, Grover Ellis shouted in pain and staggered backward against the bookcases. His face was a bright red mask.

I shoved Charity to one side and grabbed the pistol from Ellis before he could start squeezing its trigger in his death agony.

"I had to do it," Nick Wiggins said. "He was crazy. He was going to kill us all."

"But why?" Charity asked.

"For money, I suppose. He was probably in the pay of whoever's been harassing the company. Their progress must have been too slow and they decided to speed it up with murder." Nick took the still-smoking little Saturday Night Special from his pocket and, hand shaking, handed it to Ross Gautier. "I'm sorry, Chief. I know carrying this was illegal. But you can see how it was justified."

Before Gautier could answer, the whole house shook. There was the sound of wood rending and the howl of the wind as it tore open part of the wall.

"The lighthouse!" I yelled. I grabbed Charity. Lisa went ahead of us. Gautier brought up the rear, helping Jerri and keeping an eye on Nick. Margaret was jammed in between, walking solidly as if she hadn't a fear in the world.

The garage was half tumbled down. Sea water frothed around the tires of the cars. I cast a miserable look at my trusty Fleetwood. Too bad I couldn't get it inside the lighthouse, too.

197

Inside, the sound of the wind was lessened.

Gasping, Lisa said, "This is built on solid rock. If anything holds, it will."

"Upstairs," said Gautier. "The water's coming in."

It was. Creeping under the door and lapping at our feet. We climbed up the spiral staircase. It trembled under our steps.

"I should have figured you for that pistol, Nick," I said as we puffed our way toward the top. "Do you realize that by killing Ellis, you've deprived us of the chance to hear his side of the story?"

"Would you rather I'd let him shoot us all?"

"Keep climbing," I said.

We arrived at the lightroom. The old man's body was sprawled where I'd last seen it. Margaret let out a gasp and began saying a prayer. Lisa went over and looked down with no show of emotion. Then she turned and stared at me.

"It's true."

"I know." I told Nick, "There's what he wrote. See for yourself."

He looked at the scrawled name and stood up again, his face drawn and white.

In his last seconds of life, Uncle Edgar had written in ink of his own blood, "Nick."

Wiggins whirled on me. "You tricked me! You said he wrote Ellis!"

"That's right," I told him. "If we'd told you Uncle Edgar had written your name, you could have shrugged

198

it off. You're a lawyer. You know that isn't admissible evidence. But Ellis wasn't so sophisticated. He blew his cool. He also almost revealed your involvement, and that's when you killed him."

"Don't even blink, Nick," said Ross Gautier, drawing his pistol. "Ben, check his pockets, make sure he doesn't have another one of those Saturday Night Specials."

I did and he was clean.

"Why?" said Lisa. Her voice was strained as she leaned toward Nick. "It wasn't necessary! Once you'd gotten your divorce from Millie—"

"What the hell do you know?" he said harshly. "Did you really fall for that crap about breaking the trust? Sweetheart, you should have talked to another lawyer. Your old man was so slick that those Pima Indians are going to be rolling in money no matter what any of us tried to do."

"That's right," I said. "And therefore the only way to milk the company was while the girls were still alive. Or, at least one of them."

"Insurance!" said Charity.

"Right. Oh, striking oil would have been just as good —but if Dantzler Oil was to pay off rich and fast, an insurance settlement for the damage or destruction of Bugs Bunny would have served just as well."

Coldly, Lisa Dantzler said, "Do you think I was involved in anything like that?"

"No," I said. "But your sister sure was. Except that Nick made one mistake. He tried to play both ends against the middle. And Millie caught him at it. The other night was her last try at trying to save her marriage. You're right—she wouldn't have played the nude scene with anybody but Nick. But by then, Nick had decided she was expendable, and set it up to get rid of her. It's the only way it could have happened. It's just not possible that she could have come back here from Biloxi without either you *or* Nick knowing. She wanted to hide from you, because of the fact that she and her husband were preparing to loot the company. Nick picked her up and sneaked her out here to the garage, where they had a last fling and he doped her drink and sent her out to take a moonlit skin nydip. In a pool inhabited by a requiem shark."

Numbly, Lisa said, "Millie knew about us?"

"Us?" Nick parroted. "What 'us' are you referring to? Do you really believe I had any interest in you other than your bank account?"

"My God," said Charity, reaching for her purse, where she keeps the cassette recorder and also her little flat .25 automatic. She was too late.

"Don't touch it," said Jerri Marconi. She had produced a pistol of her own. "Ross, slip your gun down and let Nick take it. If you so much as blink, I'll kill Miss Tucker."

He complied.

"Too late, baby," I said to Charity. "That's the link I was missing. I've been trying to pry it out of Nick."

"Now yours, Miss Tucker."

200

Charity tossed her purse onto the floor.

"It's almost comedy," she said. "Lisa pretended to be the beard for an affair between Nick and Jerri, so she'd have a chance to be together with him. It's a double whammy. Without knowing it, Lisa really *was* the beard!"

"And the marriage license," I said. "How noble you were, Nick, showing me how you'd torn it up. But you'd already used it, hadn't you?"

He nodded. "As you said, it was in very bad taste, but what's a little bad taste in a state where first cousins are allowed to intermarry? It's all proper and legal. Jerri practiced Lisa's signature until she has it down perfect. And in case you hadn't noticed, she bears a strong resemblance to her, so if the witnesses or the justice of the peace were ever questioned later, they'd have no trouble identifying a photo of Lisa as the person they saw married to me."

"You bastard!" said Lisa. "How were you planning to dispose of me?"

"On our 'honeymoon,'" he said. "Remember the little trip I mentioned we were going to take after the funeral was over, out in the Gulf to relax? Well, you wouldn't have known it, of course, but the word would have been all over town that it was our honeymoon trip. Only at the last minute I wouldn't have gone. I'd have arranged to meet you at the first port of call, but by then, of course, the boat would have gone down mysteriously and there I'd be, widowed twice in a few days."

"You're off your gourd, Wiggins," I said. "How the hell

201

would you have gotten away with that?"

"Suspicions aren't proof," he said. "Ask the Chief here. He'll tell you."

Unhappily, Gautier said, "It might have worked. No matter what we thought, there wouldn't have been anything to tie him with the two—accidents. Ben, it happens every day."

"Listen!" said Charity.

We listened.

"I don't hear anything," I said.

"I know. The wind's died down."

"We're in the hurricane's eye," said Gautier. "It'll be calm like this for a few minutes."

"That's long enough," said Nick. "Jerri, go down and get the car started."

"What if it won't? It's built pretty low, and the water may have drowned it."

"Give me your keys, Ben," Nick said. I hesitated, and he jabbed the Chief's pistol into my belly. "Come on!"

I gave them to him. He tossed them to Jerri. "That Caddy's in the garage. It ought to go."

"You'll never get away with this," said Gautier. "Jerri, I don't know how deeply you're mixed up in it, but—"

"She's in all the way," said Nick. "She lured the shark into the pool here with that special scent. And she showed the boys down at Ballavia's Fishing Camp how to lay a trail out to the tower, to keep sharks out there, too, in case we had to shove some loudmouth overboard. Finally, she sneaked up here before the funeral and finished off Uncle

202

Edgar. So don't think you can work on her, Ross, because she's got as much to lose as I do."

I met her eyes and said, "Did you take Murder One at college, Doctor?"

"Shut up!" she spat. "What do you know about it? Were you ever a snot-nosed kid in a hick town? You bust your ass to get somewhere, and when you come back it doesn't matter where you've been or what you've done because that goddamned town hasn't changed a bit, and you're still a snot-nose." She waved her pistol at Lisa. "What do the bitches like her know, with their position and their money?" Her voice softened. "Ben, I wish it weren't you. I might—"

"Get moving," said Nick.

She went without looking back.

"What do you figure now, Nick?" asked Gautier.

"You make a guess."

"Where does your role of bereaved husband go when we're all found full of bullets?" Charity asked.

He laughed. "That won't be necessary, Miss Tucker. I reckon you've never been through one of these tropical storms."

"Once," she said.

"Well, look out there."

We craned our necks to stare out the window in the direction he pointed.

The water had receded far out into the Gulf, laying bare more than half a mile of sand and mud flats.

"The first part of the blow was offshore," Nick said.

"That pushed the waters way out there in the Gulf. But when the eye passes, the winds will reverse, and all that water will come piling back here. This whole coastline's going to go. Ask Ross. He saw one once before just like this."

Coldly, Gautier said, "Back in the forties. We lost a couple of thousand people and a row of beach houses nine miles long. He's right. The water pulled back from shore that day just the same way it's doing now."

"The lighthouse stood then," I said. "Why don't you think it will now?"

"The lighthouse wasn't in the eye then," Nick said. "It is today. What is it, Ben old buddy, do you *want* me to shoot you?" He smiled at Lisa. "Good-by, boss lady. If you ever come around this way again, you might try remembering that if you want to get something out of bed, you got to put something into it, too."

I saw Charity's hand move. Quickly, I stepped over and wrapped my arm around her shoulder, immobilizing her. She had been about to try for the tiny derringer mounted in the leather handle of her purse.

"Don't worry, baby," I said, putting on the big protective act. "He's bluffing. This lighthouse will stand."

"I'm betting it won't," said Nick Wiggins. "I've been wrong before, but the odds are on my side."

He backed toward the staircase. "Now, I'll take it mighty unkindly if any of you folks come following me down these stairs until I'm long gone." He looked out the window. "I figure we got maybe five minutes before the

204

wind comes up again and the water gets here. By then, I'll be on high land, and I reckon you all know where you'll be."

"Why," said Margaret, the maid, speaking for the first time, "you're an evil man." She stood up. "I hope you don't think a decent woman can stand by and watch you do these terrible things." She started for him.

"Margaret," I said. "Leave him alone."

She moved placidly toward him, ignoring the pistol. "It may be, Mr. Wiggins, that you can shoot me. But if you do, these gentlemen will surely fall upon you and take that revolver away from you."

"You're crazy!" he said, backing toward the stairs. "Get away."

Calmly, she said, "If what you say is true, we're going to be swept away by the storm regardless, unless we go to higher ground. So do your worst, Mr. Wiggins, and the devil take you."

Charity was the closest. She stuck out her foot and tripped poor Margaret. As she fell, Gautier caught her shoulders.

"You're a brave girl," he said. "But let him go."

"You take care, y'hear?" said Nick Wiggins as he backed down the spiral stair well.

21

W<small>E HEARD</small> Wiggins barricading the door downstairs.

"I hope you know what you're doing," said Charity.

"I'm betting that good old boy is wrong and this lighthouse will stand," I said. "The alternative seemed to be to force him to shoot us all."

"You're forgetting what I could have done with this," said Charity, slipping the derringer out of its hiding place. Ross Gautier's eyes widened.

"You folks are just plumb full of little surprises," he said. "Only thing, Miss Charity, unless you shot him right in the eye, he might still have been able to carry a few of us along with him. And I'm with Ben here. I'm betting this lighthouse will survive."

"And Mr. Wiggins won't," I said. "Not if he uses my car."

"Oh," said Charity. "Now I understand."

The wind began to rise again. The lighthouse shuddered under its force.

"Here it comes," said Lisa Dantzler, pointing at the

seaward side of the lighthouse.

Far out to sea, I saw white combers as the water rushed toward us.

"The three 'M's,'" Charity said.

"What's that?" asked Gautier.

"Money, madness and malice," said my girl. "It's bad enough to have one of them, but when all three combine, you get something like what those two"—and she nodded toward the road, where my Fleetwood was speeding toward high ground and safety—"did. Money alone isn't that important. Neither is malice. But add a touch of madness—and Mr. Nick Wiggins is bananas or my name isn't Charity Tucker—and the roof falls in."

"I hope this lighthouse holds," said Ross Gautier. "I'd admire to buy you a good drink and a better steak."

"We accept," I said.

He grinned at me. *"You,"* he said, "weren't invited."

The water was within a few hundred yards of us now. Gautier took charge. "Everybody grab onto something," he said. "Even if this thing falls down, it don't mean we're finished, not as long as we don't get swept away."

Charity and I linked arms through the metal railing around the spotlights. I saw Gautier helping Lisa and Margaret arrange themselves on the other side of the stairwell.

"Ben," Charity said.

"It's only Aunt Hilda come to visit," I said. "Please don't get sloppy sentimental."

Softly, she said, "I'm sorry about your blonde."

207

"The hell with her," I said. "She's not *my* blonde."

She kissed me. "She's not the one I meant," she whispered.

I hugged her.

It came.

The wind rose to a crescendo noise that was like every electric motor in the state turning over at full speed. The world was all tumultuous motion and violent screams of wind and rain. The heavy windows of the lighthouse shattered and horizontal torrents of water cascaded over us.

I struggled to free myself from Charity's grasp.

"We held!" I shouted.

"Ben!" she cried. "Stay down!"

"Like hell! I want to see that bastard and his no-good bitch get theirs!"

I lurched to my feet. Ross Gautier managed to stand beside me. We could see the Fleetwood, stalled just beyond the main gate to the estate. I thought I could see Nick's head poking out the driver's side. Then the other door opened and Jerri leaped out and began running frantically up the road.

A tongue of water overtook her at express-train speed. It hit the car first and tumbled it up the road. Then it clawed at her feet, her slim legs, and sucked her under.

The driving rain was like icy needles in my face. But I watched. It was a scene from a nightmare.

The water covered the graveyard, swept the church from its foundation.

Then it seemed to slow.

Now it was receding, returning to the depths from which it had been driven.

And with it came a ghastly jumble of debris.

The water had stripped the earth away from the cemetery as cleanly as a huge rake. Trees, crypts, gravestones tumbled in its wake.

And bodies.

As the water rushed seaward, it carried the inhabitants of the dead city along.

Some lodged in trees. Some huddled in ditches and against hills. Some floated past the trembling lighthouse out into the Gulf of Mexico.

I heard Lisa Dantzler moan.

"Look!" she whispered.

Near the overturned Fleetwood, a silver object floated.

It was Millie's coffin.

Slowly, it bobbed in the ebbing water, nosing against the metal of the car as if it were trying to get in. Then, finding no welcome, it drifted slowly away and out to sea.

22

THE FACE of the coast had changed.

When we came down from our shaky perch, it was to a new world.

Bodies hung suspended from trees, and first estimates were that hundreds of lives had been lost. But then it became known that most of the bodies had been swept from shallow graveyards and, although the toll of life was in the dozens, Hilda had not taken her fullest toll.

Nick Wiggins was found still clutching the steering wheel of my Fleetwood, where he had been when its twin carbs ran dry and left him stranded in the flood's path. Too bad for him that he hadn't known I had gimmicked that poor New York City car so that even if some punk managed to jump the ignition wires, he would never be able to drive it more than a block or so because of the secret cutoff valve I had installed under the seat to control gas flow. Nick, bastard that he was, still had the friendly southerner's disregard for even locking a car, and could not understand that someone else, someone like Benjamin Lincoln Shock, might not be so trusting.

Beach Row had been virtually wiped out. Where we'd seen huge old ante-bellum homes, there wasn't anything now but concrete foundations and twisted pipe. Enmeshed in one nest of pipes they found the body of Dr. Jerri Marconi, badly mangled and torn.

"Looks like a shark might of got at her," said one policeman.

I hoped not. The anger was gone now and only the packing up and leave-taking remained.

Lisa Dantzler's check was generous and included the price of a new Fleetwood to replace the old one. But I knew I could never bear to accept a younger version of my old friend.

The National Guard was ferrying people out of the disaster area, and so Charity and I left aboard a six-by-six GI truck with a dozen other refugees and, in three hours, found ourselves sitting in a New Orleans motel room.

Charity called her magic telephone and when she came back from the bathroom she was very silent.

"What do we do now?" she asked.

"I suppose you've got another job lined up."

"Maybe."

"Well, I don't want it. I'm sick of this. I'm tired of running around and I'm tired of dead people and I'm tired of—"

I stopped.

Softly, she said, "Tired of me, Ben?"

I touched her cheek. "No, baby. No. I guess I'm tired of me."

"Want to call it a day?"

It would be so easy to say "yes." But I couldn't.

"What was the phone call?" I asked.

"Some mess over in London. Forget it."

"London, England?"

"Yes. I'll call them direct and say to find someone else."

"Baby?"

"What?"

"Are *you* ready to call it a day?"

Her eyes glistened. "No, Ben."

"Then who do we see to get a passport quick?"

She smiled.

"Where are we? New Orleans?" She flipped through her address book. "I bet Harry Brooker over at CBS can help." She reached for the phone. I sighed and lay back on the bed.

"Charity?"

"Yes, sweetheart?"

"Wake me when it's time to go."